CALIFORNIA FEVER

BOOKS BY JOHN J. JACOBSON

All the Cowboys Ain't Gone
California Fever

CALIFORNIA FEVER

A NOVEL

JOHN J. JACOBSON

BLACK STONE PUBLISHING

Copyright © 2022 by John J. Jacobson
Published in 2022 by Blackstone Publishing
Cover art by Zena Kanes and Sarah Riedlinger
Cover and book design by Blackstone Publishing

The characters and events in this book are fictitious.
Any similarity to real persons, living or dead, is coincidental
and not intended by the author.

Printed in the United States of America

First edition: 2022
ISBN 978-1-6650-7162-8
Fiction / Mystery & Detective / General

Version 1

CIP data for this book is available
from the Library of Congress

Blackstone Publishing
31 Mistletoe Rd.
Ashland, OR 97520

www.BlackstonePublishing.com

In the hands of an enterprising people, what a country this might be! we are ready to say. Yet how long would a people remain so, in such a country? The Americans (as those from the United States are called) and Englishmen, who are fast filling up the principal towns, and getting the trade into their hands, are indeed more industrious and effective than the Spaniards; yet their children are brought up Spaniards, in every respect, and if the "California fever" (laziness) spares the first generation, it always attacks the second.

Richard Henry Dana Jr.,
Two Years before the Mast

CHAPTER 1

For over a month, Dolphin Smoote had been trying to get a date with the dark-eyed, willowy brunette who sat across from him in the lecture hall. But every time the six-foot, well-muscled youth with the shaggy, sun-bleached hair attempted to speak to her, his reliable cool melted like wax on a surfboard left out in the sun. Dolphin wasn't accustomed to falling apart in front of attractive young women or doing such un-casual things.

Her name was Claudette, and she had caught Dolphin's attention at a series of summer lectures given at Beach Cities Community College, which wasn't far from his home in Tranquility Beach, Southern California. He was attending a course entitled The Power of Positive Dreaming because he thought he might learn how to get rich without having to work very hard. After a session, Dolphin would try to casually saunter up to where she sat and start a conversation. Yet after one look into her eyes, which reminded him of fizzy root beer, he'd fall apart. His carefully planned words couldn't get past his pulsing Adam's apple, which was following the rapid beat of his heart.

Unfortunately, he wore a Saint Christopher medal on a choker, which accordingly danced a jig on his neck. This was further distracting to him, and probably to her too. Soon, sweat would bead on his upper lip and forehead. He ended up sounding like he was trying to get a point across with his tongue glued to the top of his mouth. Alas, when Love's arrow truly lands, who can resist the effect?

If Dolphin hadn't been so much in love, he would have been ashamed. For "whacking out" in front of a girl was a serious breach of classic, old-time surfer style, and maintaining that classic surfer style was what Dolphin and his friends were all about. He was from Tranquility Beach, after all, one of the two or three places where the phenomenon all began, and in the early summer of 1988, where it still lingered.

For the Dawgs (short for Surf Dawgs, as Dolphin and his friends called themselves), style could be reduced to two primary qualities, both of which were legacies from the early days of Southern California surf culture. The first of these qualities was the art of being "casual." Surf legends like Mickey Dora and Lance Carson used to perform stunts like riding the noses of their surfboards and hanging five or ten, all while making it look so effortless that the only possible way to have been more casual would have been to be asleep. It was Dolphin who usually out-casualed the other Surf Dawgs. Even so, Dolphin's adamantine walls of casual and cool crumbled like soda crackers before Claudette and her sparkling eyes, demonstrating again that one of the most powerful forces under the sun is a beautiful woman.

Casual wasn't the only quality Dolphin and the Dawgs valued. They aspired also to be "radical." This meant being insanely fearless. A true Dawg sought to perform the most daring stunts imaginable, both on and off their surfboards. This could be going over hundred-foot cliffs on their recently invented snowboards, riding their skateboards down the steep hairpin curves of Palos Verdes, climbing the two-hundred-foot radar towers in Portuguese Bend, doing rollercoasters off the lips of closed-out waves, hanging back in the curl on big hollow waves, late paddle takeoffs on big, elevator-shaft-steep waves, et cetera. But radical could never be separated from casual. These insanities were to be done in the most nonchalant way, as if they were as commonplace as going to work, though that was very un-commonplace for Dolphin and his friends.

The greatest casual-radical of them all was SC Parker. Dolphin idolized SC for the totally insane stunts he was reputed to have done, such as riding tornado surf in the Midwest and surfing a huge wave on a river in Tennessee that had been caused by a dynamited dam. But what particularly settled Dolphin's hero worship of SC was the fact that the house in which Dolphin lived with his aunt Clementine was the very house that years ago SC had grown up in.

One can imagine Dolphin's absolute confusion when he would repeatedly gag on his words to a mere girl, making noises like an annoying, squealing seal. But as suggested, radical was also deeply embedded in his character, and radical meant that he couldn't let himself "hair out." Dolphin Smoote wasn't about to give up on Claudette.

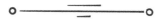

The morning after his latest fiasco in attempting to get a date with Claudette, Dolphin went surfing. The waves had been fairly good four- and five-footers, and the sun was shining with a slight offshore breeze coming from the southeast. But instead of tearing it up in the water until it got choppy, Dolphin stayed out for less than an hour. He retreated from the water and sat on his surfboard on the beach, contemplating his situation and watching the seagulls pick at the sand crabs. Then he had an inspiration. He would take his problem to Lunch Biggunes.

Lunch Biggunes was the Dawgs' mentor, a semi-legendary surfer himself, about twenty years older than Dolphin. Lunch's given name was Roland, and those who saw Lunch now in his maturity might incorrectly assume his nickname was a reference to his girth. Rather, Lunch had gotten his sobriquet for the tremendous wipeouts of his former days—"eating lunch" as it is called. Lunch would regularly take off on incredibly humungous waves, in impossible positions. The name Lunch really was a dubbing; he was a true knight of the ocean.

Just south of the stately old house on the Strand, where Dolphin lived with his aunt Clementine, was the Tranquility Beach pier. From the Strand—the concrete walkway and bike path that bordered the beach—the pier extended 70 yards over the beach and stretched another 150 yards out over the ocean. It was supported by heavy concrete pilings on either side, set ten yards apart. In the '60s and early '70s, before it was outlawed, a most radical stunt was to "shoot the pier"—that is, while being propelled on an unpredictable wave, maneuvering through the gnarly, barnacled pilings while standing on a slab of foam wrapped in fiberglass and resin.

Dolphin found Lunch under the Tranquility Beach pier, where he was currently residing in a camp halfway between the Strand and the water. When Dolphin walked up, Lunch was sitting on a beach chair leaning over his small Weber grill.

"She turned me down," Dolphin explained to Lunch, "with some of the best excuses I've ever heard, and with a few that weren't so hot." Dolphin flopped down cross-legged on the soft sand. "Once she told me she had to stay home so she could re-arrange her sock drawer. I'm sure she thinks I'm a total kook." For the uninitiated, *kook* is the technical term for a person who tries to surf but is lame at it, and whose trying lacks style—that is, their attempts are neither casual nor radical.)

"She must not be from around here if she thinks you're a kook, dude," said Lunch as he casually grilled bratwursts on his barbeque. "Anybody from around here could tell you're a Dawg and not a kook." He rolled one of the sausages over with his bare fingers, slightly burning himself.

"Thanks, Lunch, but that doesn't help. You're right, though—she's from the Midwest or someplace like that."

"The Midwest!" Lunch moaned, removing his burnt fingers from his mouth. "What do you see in her?"

"She's tall like a model. Matter of fact, I heard her tell some-one she *is* a model. She's got these awesome big brown eyes that for some reason remind me of root beer. And she's . . ."

"What?"

"It's called *aloof.* You know—she doesn't care about the normal things girls care about."

"You mean you?"

"She doesn't even know my name."

"Makes you want them even more." Lunch took one of the sausages off the grill and put it in a bun. "Sure you don't want one of these?" Lunch asked before he took a sizable bite.

"Man, I'm appetiteless."

Dolphin's not wanting a bratwurst concerned Lunch, causing him to dig deep into his vast experience with women. "What you need, dawg," Lunch went on after masticating the bite, "is leverage. Exactly what I *don't* have at the moment with Nicole." Nicole was Lunch's twenty-something-year-old girlfriend. Being an almost surf legend did have its rewards, however tenuous.

"You mean that's why she threw your stuff out on the bike path?" asked Dolphin, referring to the event that had led to Lunch's dwelling under the pier.

"Yep, that's it. Leverage."

"How can I get some?"

"You already got it."

"I do?"

"You do."

"What is it?"

Lunch spread his arms and looked all around him. "The beach, dawg. You got the beach."

CHAPTER 2

Finally, as is not always the case in matters of the heart, Dolphin's persistence paid off. Following Lunch's counsel, he invited Claudette to the beach. After a dialogue that challenged Dolphin considerably, she agreed to have lunch with him that upcoming Saturday afternoon. Lunch had told him he had to forget about style when he talked to her. That would come later. "Just get the words out—that's all you need to care about," he'd instructed. "Just barf 'em out if you have to."

That Wednesday night, after their class, Dolphin had approached Claudette, having removed his Saint Christopher medal.

"Do you want to come down to the beach one of these days? I live there," Dolphin said in one rapid spurt of words.

To this, Claudette's eyebrows curled up a quarter inch or so. "I don't think I even know your name. Why would I want to do that?"

"I live down on the Strand in Tranquility. It's pretty cool down there."

"I like going to the beach when it's hot," she said.

"Tranquility Beach is cool even when it's hot," he spurted again, "and cool even when it's not hot."

"That makes a lot of sense," she said. "I've heard of Tranquility Beach. Isn't that where all the eccentrics live?"

"It's not like the Beach Cities closer to LA. Some of my friends want to put up barbed wire and machinegun nests to keep the Vals and New Yorkers out."

Pondering this last statement for a few moments, she then asked, "And just what is a Val?"

"It's people from the San Fernando Valley—kooks and hodads, you know, people who can't surf."

"Sounds like you have a bunch of lunatic criminals for friends." The room had nearly emptied of all students, and Claudette started gathering her things off her desk.

"Not all of them, they're just surfers and want to keep the surf to themselves." He had meant to just say, "not at all." Dolphin could feel his throat pounding again. He tried to explain, "They're nothing compared to Crazy Ahab and the Village Idiots or the Wave Nazis"

Claudette laughed. "Like I said, sounds like Tranquility Beach is overflowing with lunatic criminals."

"It's not like that," Dolphin stammered, but he was happy that at least he was getting words out, even if they lacked style. "They're a group of lame surfers who try to make up for it by calling themselves weird names. They don't rate at all. The Wave Nazis are actually from El Porto, anyway. Crazy Ahab and the Idiots don't rate either. They're from Manhattan Beach." He saw that this last statement didn't have the desired effect and tried to clear up the confusion: "Crazy Ahab and the Village Idiots are a bunch of kooks from the beach next to ours. I'm from T Beach, and T Beach is different."

"Well, *you* certainly are," she said. She had packed her large purse, which now hung from her shoulder. She reached in and pulled from it a small tape recorder. She pushed a button and spoke into it. "Tonight I had the pleasure of meeting Crazy Ahab, one of the Village Idiots, from . . ."

"No, no," he said, dropping the notebook he had not taken any notes in, "I'm Dolphin Smoote, from Tranquility Beach. And it really is awesome down there. It's still like the Beach Cities used to be thirty years ago. You know, slow and mellow and fun."

Up to this point, Claudette hadn't been so much interested as amused. But now, she clicked off her tape recorder and gave Dolphin an inquiring look. "Dolphin Smoote. What a curious name."

"My real name is Randy," Dolphin said, avoiding the whole truth—his name was actually Randolph, something he wouldn't confess even under torture—"but my friends all call me Dolphin," and added, trying to be humble, "'cause I'm pretty good in the water."

"Do you spell Smoote with an *e*?" Claudette asked.

"No, two *o*'s," said Dolphin.

Claudette almost seemed disappointed.

And then Dolphin made the calculation. "I mean, yeah, two *o*'s and an *e* at the end."

After a thoughtful pause, Claudette said, "Well, I would love to. When should I come?"

Dolphin dared to look up at that face. Her gorgeous, full, dark-brown eyebrows had arched another millimeter or two, and there was something like the hint of a smile on her face. Maybe, he thought, he was finally getting his style back.

CHAPTER 3

Dolphin's 1974 Land Cruiser, though recently repaired, was still waiting to be picked up at Van's Service Station. After Dolphin peppered his aunt Clemmie with deft reasonings and pleadings, she had coughed up the money to get it fixed. Dolphin, however, had succumbed in turn to his friend Chip Thomas's own pleading and deft reasoning and lent the money so Chip could pay the rent on his surf shop and keep it from closing down. The Land Cruiser thus remained in the shop, and Dolphin felt relieved when Claudette asked for directions, realizing he was saved from picking her up. She even made a joke about getting past the barbed wire and machinegun nests. He gave her directions to a quaint little café a couple of blocks from his house.

Quaint in the context of his description of the café could have had a variety of meanings. In this case, it was a cover for a place that he thought might impress Claudette while not being too expensive. This café, like the town itself, retained the ambiance of the old laid-back Southern California surf culture Dolphin had tried to describe to Claudette. By the early '80s, transients from the East and Midwest had smothered out much of the old lifestyle in the Beach Cities near Los Angeles. But this was not true of T Beach, as Tranquility Beach was called by those in the know, or at Surf Burgers, where Claudette was to meet Dolphin. They would have lunch there, stroll out on the pier, and maybe down the Strand in the opposite direction from his house. Dolphin's plan for the afternoon was to avoid two things: one was the beach boutiques that cluttered the east side of Pacific Avenue. In a matter of seconds, a guy could blow beaucoup dollars trying to impress a new love. The other was his aunt Clemmie. This meant avoiding his house, or to be more precise, Aunt Clemmie's house, where he was a rent-free boarder when she wasn't too upset with him.

Saturday finally came. There had been good waves in the morning. The early afternoon sun wasn't too hot. A slight but pleasant onshore breeze came in from the west. And Claudette was apparently enjoying her lunch at Surf Burgers. Very few can resist the Rat Beach Burger Melt with grilled onions and cheddar on cracked sourdough bread. Dolphin was a little surprised—and, frankly, a little concerned—at how much she was eating, though. He shuddered at the idea that dating her could get expensive. He had hoped she, being a model and all, would only order a small salad and a diet coke.

Other than Claudette enjoying the food, the date wasn't going that great. Dolphin had tried to show interest in Claudette's work. He had talked over his coming date with Lunch Biggunes, and Lunch's advice was to ask a lot of questions. But every statement or inquiry he made was crashing hard to earth, like the time he fell off his aunt Clemmie's roof trying to install a spotlight so he could surf at night.

"Can I ask you a question?" Dolphin said when the well of his imagination about modeling was pretty much dried up.

"Go ahead," Claudette replied, after swallowing a bite of her burger.

"Do you ever get the urge to just dive off one of those runways, like leap off into the crowd? That would be so radical."

"I'll answer it if it's the last one you ask about modeling. I don't like modeling. I hate modeling. I only do it part time, and only because I have to," she said, and downed the last of her vanilla shake.

"Oh," Dolphin said, figuring modeling must not pay much. He hoped she wasn't now going to order desert.

"I'm not a runway type of model, anyway. I'm only what they call a 'fit model.' Occasionally I'll also do a store catalog."

"Oh, cool! Is that because you're in really good shape?"

"You said you wouldn't ask any more questions."

"Oh."

"It's where I try on the new styles, so the salespeople can see them on a live person and see if the clothes are true to size. Get it? See if the clothes 'fit.' I am a perfect size."

Dolphin said, "I totally agree." He was tempted not to say it, but Dawgs don't hair out.

"What?"

"Nothing. Why don't you like modeling? I wouldn't mind getting paid for just wearing clothes." He thought about saying something else, but this time he did hair out.

"I hate modeling."

"Why do you do it then?"

"To support myself until . . . until"—she hesitated—"until I can get my other career going."

"What other career?"

"I don't like talking about it."

"Why?"

"It's bad luck."

"What's bad luck?"

"Talking about doing what I want to be doing before I'm doing it."

"Oh." This left Dolphin pondering, nodding his head for a few moments. He suddenly realized he was talking about something she wanted to talk about. He saw the corners of her mouth flexing up slightly. Another almost smile! A flash of inspiration struck him—Apollo or whoever that god was, was on the loose—she wanted to talk about the thing she said she didn't want to talk about! She *did* have some similarities to a normal girl.

She looked about the room at the walls covered with old pictures of old surf legends she'd never heard of—Greg Noll, Dewey Weber, Lance Carson, Mike Purpose, Mickey Dora, Corky Carroll—and an almost hum started easing out of her mouth. She was waiting for Dolphin to ask something, and this time he tried to handle his words delicately.

"So, what's it you really want to do?" he said, not that delicately but amazed at how freely it had come to him. Chemistry! Timing! And she was beautiful and took the Power of Positive Dreaming classes and was not a complete hodad. She was aloof and smart and didn't mind coming down to the beach to visit him. Her only flaw was that she ate so much, which was expensive, but maybe that could just be attributed to the ocean air and the food at Surf Burgers.

"Ohhh," she dawdled. "You wouldn't be interested."

"I might be," said Dolphin, immediately realizing this reply lacked something.

"Besides," she said, "I told you some writers think it's bad luck to talk about their writing too early in their development."

"Oh! I see. You want to be a writer. There's nothing the matter with that. I used to write a surf column in the *T Beach Weekly*. It ran for a couple of months," Dolphin said, rounding up. The column only lasted three editions, even though they had been quite good. Aunt Clemmie had even praised them. But a big south swell hit Mexico a few days before the next deadline, and Dolphin and his buddies took off in his Land Cruiser for Lower Baja, causing Dolphin to flake out on the column.

"Well, it's really not that important," Claudette said, blushing and looking down at the remaining crumbs of her onion rings.

"What kind of stuff do you want to write?" Dolphin asked. By the way her head sprang up and the fire he saw in her eyes, he knew the inspiration was back with him.

"Mysteries, detective stories, crime thrillers—I'm wild about crime."

"Well, then you would probably like my aunt Clemmie," Dolphin said. "She writes crime stories." He immediately realized he was off the mark on this one. He should have said you might be *interested* in my aunt Clemmie, for even with his theory of the elasticity of truth, it would be inaccurate to say that anyone could *like* his aunt.

"You have an aunt who's a crime writer? What has she written?"

"About fifty-seven books, I guess, maybe more. She keeps popping them out, like a"—here Dolphin paused because he was going to say "like a rabbit makes bunnies," but something held him back. He finally came up with an alternative—"like weeds." This didn't make a whole lot of sense either.

"Wait a minute," Claudette exclaimed, jumping up from her seat. "You aren't saying that Clementine Hardin is your aunt, are you?"

"Every cloud has its dark lining," Dolphin said, trying to be a little literary himself. "And she's mine."

"I knew she lived in one of the Beach Cities, but for some reason I thought she was British. And your last name's Smoote isn't it."

"Yeah, and it's hers too. Hardin's her writing name. Her great-grandfather, and my great-great-grandfather, was some Old West outlaw named Hardin, and she likes to use that name on her books."

"Yes, John Wesley Hardin, the famous gunslinger outlaw. I've read all about him."

"For some reason she's really proud of us having him for an ancestor, even if he plugged thirty-plus dudes or so. She says having a criminal in the bloodline is why she's such a good crime writer."

"I absolutely adore Clementine Hardin. Someday I'm going to be just like her."

This last statement gave Dolphin a jolt, and for a moment he thought Claudette was out of her mind, perhaps from all the sugar in the shake or the grease on the onion rings. He had a momentary vision of being chained to a woman like Aunt Clemmie for life and almost lost consciousness. That would be a definite no-op.

But then, taking another look at those eyes and the brows that shaded them, he realized this must just be her artistic nature

coming through. Aunt Clemmie called it the "poetic temperament" when she stretched the truth or did other weird stuff.

"Well, if you really want to meet her, I think she's home
now," Dolphin said, without taking the time to think this all
the way through. That had been one of the things he wanted to
avoid. "At least she was there disturbing the peace this morning."

"You mean I could meet her? I would be your friend for-
ever if you introduced me!" And with that, she sprang over at
Dolphin and grabbed his face with both hands and kissed him
squarely on the lips.

CHAPTER 4

The walk from Surf Burgers to Aunt Clemmie's house was less than a half mile. To arrive at the front of the house—the most impressive view of her impressive domicile—one would walk one block north on Tranquility Avenue and make a left down Grunion Lane, the side street. Then, upon reaching the bike path fronting the beach, one would walk north up the concrete path thirty more yards, turn ninety degrees, and be looking at the front of the stately old beach house Aunt Clemmie called home.

The locals called it the Sandcastle. And it didn't take much imagination to see that it really was a huge replica of one of those creations that would-be architects occasionally build down in the wet sand. It was very large for a beach house, a sand-brown stucco structure of seven thousand square feet, three stories, three balconies, five bedrooms, a cellar, and maid's and butler's quarters. The latter two rooms were seldom used, as Aunt Clemmie was too cheap to hire full-time help and would have worked them to death if she did.

The house was built in the late 1920s by a wealthy eccentric to look like an ominous, fortified castle. Balustrades all the way round, barred arched windows, and a very large and heavy wooden front door that suggested a portcullis all contributed to the stately effect. The castle had almost everything but a moat, which Dolphin thought would have been the coolest feature of all. But moats don't obstruct the type of intruders this house was designed to keep out. The house was in truth designed to thwart ghosts. Not even one ninety-degree angle was to be found in any of its internal walls. Because of the not-so-well-known fact that ghosts like to hang out in such nooks, all the internal walls met in rounded plaster corners.

The Sandcastle was a famous landmark in T Beach, for the old place itself was as unique as the current owner. Aunt Clemmie had it meticulously restored to its original state when she bought it some twenty years earlier, after *Blood on the Beach* had become her first big-selling book.

"You live *here*? My goodness!" Claudette said upon their arrival at the front door.

"Life's not always as peachy as it looks," Dolphin said.

"No, really, it must be fantastic."

"Aunt Clemmie travels quite a bit, and let me tell you, we've had some awesome parties. Usually I get caught, but no need to mention any of that to her."

"I'll be on my very best behavior. I promise."

Dolphin took a big breath as they walked up to the huge front door and said, "She is quite formal, and likes to be called Ms. Clementine by my friends. I am the only one she allows to call her Aunt Clemmie. No curtsy necessary, but she likes a slight bow of the head. And one other thing: don't disagree with her. She doesn't like that. And of course, you wouldn't ever say anything negative about her writing. Got it?"

"Got it," Claudette said. "I don't know what I'm going to do to ever thank you."

"Don't worry about it. She'll probably think I'm coming up in the world, having a friend who's literate."

Stepping inside the house, the two immediately ran into six or seven large suitcases sitting in the entryway. These side-stepped, they walked into the living room just in time to behold Aunt Clemmie making a rapid and noisy, though somehow majestic, march down the elegantly curved stairway. The room into which she descended was large and smartly decorated in a 1930s art deco style and had an almost floor-to-ceiling picture window that, when not shuttered, gave an unobstructed view of the ocean.

A creditable chronicler of California life in the mid-1800s made the statement quoted at the beginning of this story, inferring that something in the very land and climate of Southern California tends to infect its inhabitants with a marked disinclination to gainful employment. That Harvard-educated author described it as the "California Fever." And though that characterization definitely applied to Aunt Clemmie's nephew and his friends, it would be quite unfit to lay it upon her. She was, without exaggeration, a hurricane of energy, activity, and productivity.

Her movement down the stairway was one of those serendipitous events that those of the artistic temperament often seem to provoke. It was blustery but somehow majestic, like a large, plump fairy godmother promenading to earth. She was dressed in a semiformal gown that hung loosely over her line-backeresque frame. A triple string of pearls bounded on her over-ample bosom. A gaudy purple hat—a women's version of a 1930s fedora—too small for her, adorned her size 7⅝ head. Except for its color, the hat might have come out of a noir gangster movie. The hat only partially concealed her dyed red hair. To finish the picture, a small Maltese snuggled under her right arm. She was urging along a young woman, dressed fashionably in a pant suit, who was following behind her, carrying three more pieces of luggage.

"Oh, there you are, my indolent young reprobate," she said not unkindly upon seeing Dolphin and taking no notice of Claudette. "It's good you are here. Now I won't have to send Julia searching the barren wastes for you."

Seeing she was in a good mood, Dolphin breathed easier. Whenever she called him anything with a *my* preceding it, it portended sunny skies, at least for the next few moments.

"Are you going somewhere, Auntie?" Dolphin asked.

"Hurry child, Time is brandishing his scythe," Aunt Clemmie said, addressing the young woman with the luggage. Before Time could even begin to heft his scythe again, Aunt Clemmie turned and with the dexterity of an ibex bounded up five steps to where the girl seemed to be stuck. Aunt Clemmie grabbed two of the pieces with her free hand and shooed the girl back up the stairs. Without discomforting the Maltese, she grabbed the third piece with her not-so-free hand and started down the stairs.

Dolphin, late in his effort, started up the stairs to help, but by the time he got to the second step, Aunt Clemmie was there too. Their collision, though minor, was not pretty. Aunt Clemmie's good mood, however, was not shaken, for all she noticed was that Dolphin actually tried to help. "That was decent of you, boy. I take back 'reprobate,' which I just said of you—but not 'indolent.'"

"Why all the luggage, Auntie? I thought you were going to

be here for the summer. Or are you just giving Julia some exercise? Running in the soft sand is good too, you know."

"What is holding that girl up?" Aunt Clemmie said, not bothering with Dolphin's questions or wisecracks, to which she was annealed. "Would you please go up there and help her with my bags already. I haven't got all day."

Dolphin started up the stairs about half as fast as his aunt had, but she followed hard after him goading him along.

"Easy," he said. "You're harshing my mellow."

"That's not all I'll be harshing if you don't cut out that abominable surf-speak. *Harsh* is not a verb."

"You told me Shakespeare turned nouns into verbs all the time. The dude who wanted to just 'sit on the ground and tell sad stories about the deaths of kings,' wanted his friends to 'unking' him."

"*Harsh* is an adjective, you blockhead. But you're not nearly as stupid as you let on to be. If you just weren't so lazy."

Dolphin snorted. "I'm not lazy, just selective in what I do."

Apparently, Aunt Clemmie didn't have time to answer this and, at the third level of the stairs, broke off and sped down a hallway.

After a few minutes, Dolphin and Aunt Clemmie were back in the living room, the latter apparently satisfied she wasn't going to run out of clothes wherever she was going. Claudette had stepped over to get a closer view of the contents of one of the bookcases.

"Why the big hurry, Auntie?" Dolphin asked again.

"No hurry, no hurry. I just like getting the difficult tasks, the ones I don't care for, out of the way. It's the secret of my productivity. Always do what you are least inclined to do first."

Dolphin thought of mentioning that it wasn't she alone

who was doing the difficult task of hauling a half ton of luggage down three flights of stairs but refrained.

Checking the large Breitling she wore on her wrist, Aunt Clemmie said, "Now let's have tea, before I have to leave. And then you can introduce me to your friend."

Dolphin and Claudette followed Aunt Clemmie into the dining room. As Dolphin was trying to remember the proper order in formal introductions, Aunt Clemmie jumped up and darted out of the room.

After a few minutes, Julia brought in tea and scones and, setting them on the table, whispered to Dolphin, "We're going to New York." Julia, Aunt Clemmie's assistant was herself a T Beach local whose family had a house on the Strand down the beach. She had recently graduated from UCLA, and Dolphin was the one who got her the job as Aunt Clemmie's assistant.

After a few more minutes, Aunt Clemmie flew back in and, not waiting for Dolphin, took care of the introduction herself.

"Claudette is one of your biggest fans, Auntie. She's also a writer. She wants to be just like you and write crime thrillers."

"I don't write crime thrillers, you boob. I am a poet who sings the tragedies of distempered souls," she said, and seemed to drift off somewhere in her imagination.

"Sorry, I keep on forgetting," said Dolphin.

"Claudette Leaf," Aunt Clemmie said repeating Claudette's full name and looking her over. "Interesting name, Ms. Leaf. Where did you say you're from?"

"She didn't," Dolphin chimed in. "She lives in Westwood."

"Clamp it, please," said Aunt Clemmie, who was a stickler for all forms of decorum, and would never say, "shut up." Her large vocabulary didn't require the word.

Claudette took this as an invitation to speak. "I was born in Oklahoma. My family moved to Texas when I was twelve, and I've been in California now for three months. I do so much admire your writing—I'm using yours as a model for mine."

"Cookson Hills, Oklahoma, I would venture?" Aunt Clemmie said.

"That's where my grandmother lives. I was actually born in Tulsa. How did you know?"

"I knew it! Your nose has just a slight crook in it, just as his did. Randy, my young slacker, unless I am deceived, your friend here is the great-great-granddaughter of none other than Charles Arthur Floyd, better known as Pretty Boy Floyd."

Dolphin was moderately impressed. He had heard of the old outlaw. Claudette was dumbfounded.

"I've studied Pretty Boy extensively," Aunt Clemmie explained. "In my third book, *The Missing Earlobe*, I had a character based upon him. Pretty Boy had a daughter whose name was Claudette also, and she married Leroy Leaf, who was also a bank robber, though small time—don't believe he whacked anyone. That's your pedigree, young Ms. Leaf."

"I never knew . . ." Claudette stuttered.

"She's one of the 'scattered leaves,'" said Aunt Clemmie, clapping her hands together and exploding in an eruption of laughter, in which Dolphin didn't join.

"Oh, it's so trying having to explain my jokes to him," she went on after her paroxysm passed, "I am sure, Ms. Leaf, you know your Dante: 'In its depths I saw entangled, bound by love in one volume, the scattered leaves of all the universe.'"

"Actually, that's a pretty good one, Auntie," Dolphin said.

"I don't know if you have the talent, Ms. Leaf, but you do

have a bloodline. Of course, it's nothing like mine: thirty-two killings, banks, trains—John Hardin even robbed a few temperance meetings. Charles Floyd was nothing compared to that, but still nothing to be ashamed of."

"But Auntie," broke in Dolphin, "Didn't great-great-grandpa always say he didn't plug anyone who didn't deserve plugging?"

"Bunch of blather, child. Of course he would say that—criminals have to rationalize their crimes. That's why the blood is so essential: if you want to write crime, you have to think like a criminal, feel like a criminal. And it is the blood that feeds the mind and heart. Therefore, if you want to think and feel like a criminal, you need the blood. Simple logic, you know."

"Thank you so much for the encouragement," Claudette said.

"My pleasure, and do call me Aunt Clemmie. And let me know if there is anything I can do for you. I always want to encourage young people. Though with him," she said, alluding to Dolphin, "it's like encouraging sand. Now, I must put my mind to other things." Aunt Clementine called to Julia.

After Dolphin gave up thinking how he was like sand, his agile mind started contemplating how it was that Aunt Clemmie had warmed to Claudette so quickly. What bothered him most was not that Aunt Clemmie was so friendly to Claudette. Instead, he got a creeping sense that Claudette seemed to care more about Aunt Clemmie than for him. It might have started harshing his mellow again, but during the conversation, his mind had been started on something else: Julia had mentioned New York, and there had of course been lots of luggage. That was always a good thing.

"So, Auntie, are you rushing out of here to join the FBI? You've kinda captured the G-man look."

Aunt Clemmie finally gave up some information. "I got a call from my agent this morning, and it turns out that the studio wants to pay, oh, I won't be so boorish to tell you how much." Here she started laughing again, and after a few seconds she recovered and went on: "To adapt my novel, *Red Hair, Red Blood* for the screen."

Dolphin added to Claudette, "Her book is about the tendencies red-haired people have for mayhem. That's why Aunt Clemmie's hair is currently red. She likes getting into character."

"Well, I am going to Manhattan for the summer. They tried to get me to do the work in Hollywood, but you know how I feel about those reprobates. Nothing worse than criminals without art or taste. And besides, the producer I will be working with lives there. So, I get my Manhattan, and he gets his script. The one proviso is that I must be there in a week, and you know how I feel about flying. My train departs at eight o'clock tonight."

"Then, you have five hours," said Dolphin.

"Nonsense. I will have lots to do when I get to the station."

A frightening thought hit Dolphin. Was she going to ask him to drive her to the train station? "I don't know if all that luggage is going to fit in my car," he said, trying to ward off that potential unpleasantness.

"I am not going to ride in that rattrap of yours. The studio is sending a limousine. It should be here shortly."

Dolphin relaxed.

"I talked with Sam the grocer and he will make deliveries twice a week. My accountant will take care of the utilities, as always. I am not leaving you with any cash for anything else. You've got to learn to be self-sufficient. And this summer should be a good test."

At this point, Julia came into the room. "The car is here, Ms. Clementine."

Dolphin and Claudette walked Aunt Clemmie into the front room, where the limousine driver was toiling with the luggage. Dolphin suggested someone ought to give him a hand, hating to see anybody work so hard. But Aunt Clemmie had other thoughts. "Let him do his job," she said. "Demeaning a man's pride leads to malfeasance."

"Oh!" Claudette reached into her purse. "I've been reading one of your books, and I wonder if you would sign it for me." She pulled out a first edition and handed it to Aunt Clemmie. "I always carry a Hardin with me," she said to Dolphin.

Aunt Clemmie gave the book the once- or twice-over, then did the same to Claudette. "A first edition of my *Massacre at the Picnic*."

"You never know when you're going to have idle moments," Claudette said.

"Crime is not a picnic and doesn't pay. Best wishes, C. Hardin," Aunt Clemmie mouthed as she signed.

Aunt Clemmie then donned her trench coat, and with her fedora could have a passed for a G-man in a surrealistic retro nightmare. Dolphin kissed her cheek, and in a moment, she was out the front door. Suddenly, her red-haired, felt-hatted head popped back in the doorway. "No parties, Randolph, and in no way use these premises for any of your ill-advised activities." With that, she departed.

"She is just wonderful," Claudette said to Dolphin. "Thank you so much. It has been such a fun day."

"You liked her, huh?" He was thinking again about the attention she'd shown to Aunt Clemmie rather than to him. But there was *some* good news at least. Dolphin realized that he had begun to relax around her. He wasn't back to his natural casual-radical self, but at least he could talk, more or less, without tripping over his larynx.

"If you aren't doing anything, you could drive me back to Westwood," Claudette said sweetly. "And we could go out to dinner."

Dinner, Dolphin thought. *She wouldn't want to go out to dinner with someone she thought was a toad. Well, maybe if the toad was paying for it.* But Dolphin couldn't accept. "My garage is still in the car," he said.

Claudette's expression changed to looking like she was trying to hold back a big sneeze. "Your garage is in the car?" she asked.

"I mean, my car's in the garage. It broke down. It had a bad valve."

"Well, then, would you walk me to the bus stop? My car is in the garage too."

"We have a lot in common," Dolphin said, smiling.

"We do, don't we," she said. And they went off looking for the bus stop, which Dolphin didn't have a clue where to find.

CHAPTER 5

If Dolphin's mellow was only partially shaken before, on the way back from walking Claudette to the bus stop, it took a further plunge. He felt like his eyes were rolling around one way in their sockets before screeching to halt and rolling back the other way and, like Sherman's cavalry, had detoured through his stomach on their way to the sea. Thoughts of Claudette's sparkling brown eyes almost got him run over by a bike rider on one of the side streets. Then thoughts of his sorry financial condition rushed on.

Dolphin had been searching for the words to ask her if he could see her again, when surprisingly, *she* asked if they could get together again next weekend. Dolphin managed a yes without much difficulty. She suggested he take her to a murder-mystery dinner theater in Santa Monica. When she asked if his car would be ready by then and if he could pick her up, he, for some reason, said "not a problem." Love with this girl, no doubt, was going to be expensive. At least on the way to the bus she didn't ask him to stop at Surf Burgers and buy her a piece of chocolate cream pie.

It was Saturday, and the date was set for next Friday night. By his calculation, he had less than a week to raise the $789 to get his car out of the garage, and whatever else it was going to cost to take Ms. Dream Girl out to wine and dine at the dinner theater, which wasn't cheap either. And why did she have to pick a dinner theater? Couldn't they just go to dinner? or to the theater? But to a dinner theater! Two dates in one—it would probably cost twice as much.

Some say football is a microcosm of life. That is, there are moral and spiritual lessons that can be gathered from playing the game, such as getting up off the turf and going at it again after being repeatedly knocked down by a 300-pound defensive end who runs the forty in 4.5 seconds and can bench press 520 pounds. But football is a child's doodle picture compared to surfing. And to the sport of kings, Dolphin now mentally fled for strength and wisdom. The challenges he now felt, he tried to convince himself, were really nothing compared to a late paddle take off at low tide on a fifteen-foot wave at Lunada Bay Point. Surfing those waves, it was possible to end up on the jagged rocks looming twenty feet in front of him if he didn't make a clean takeoff. With waves this steep, he had to weight the tail of his board just enough so he wouldn't pearl—but not too much, or the nose of the board would float and he couldn't get the speed to beat the lip to the bottom and would get crunched going over the falls and smashing onto the shallow rocks. And after surviving the drop and shooting out of his bottom turn, a false section over ten feet high would likely pop up in front of him, so he'd have to get enough speed by jamming to the top before cutting back off the lip and blasting out of another bottom turn fast enough to outrun it. And adding to this, there's

Crazy Ahab and four or five Village Idiots out in the water at the same time, thinking they own the whole fricking ocean and totally pissed at him because he just got the wave of the day, so they're thinking up ways they can cause him to die. What are the challenges of love and lucre compared to this?

Dolphin reconsidered, and realized Lunada Bay at fifteen feet was a piece of that chocolate cream pie at Surf Burgers, compared to the fix he was now in. Dolphin decided he needed once again to take his problems to Lunch Biggunes.

It was surely a slip of the tongue when Aunt Clemmie used the qualifier "ill-advised" when admonishing Dolphin about possible activities in her house while she was gone. That was the trouble with being a writer. She tended to be verbose, sometimes using words just for their own sake, a tendency with which many writers are plagued. But for better or for worse, she *had* used the phrase. And as Dolphin walked down the Strand toward Lunch's hangout, Aunt Clemmie's statement stirred in the deep cavities of his mind. Then suddenly it exited those deep cavities, and inspiration struck.

Ill-advised! As long as it wasn't "ill-advised," he might be able to use the Sandcastle to make his sorely needed dough. On his own, he might not have thought of using the house for any kind of venture, but as fate would have it, the suggestion had been presented to him. As long as it wasn't "ill-advised," and of course, that would be up to the eye of the beholder.

A moment after this thought came to him, he saw a sign on a beach house a few doors down the Strand.

CHAPTER 6

Cocktail hour had arrived at Lunch's hangout under the pier. The Dawgs called it so, not because they began drinking cocktails at 5:00 p.m., for they didn't. But if the waves didn't look like they were going to be good in the early-evening glass-off, they did generally gather around that time and would, on occasion, tip a few, though typically just beer or wine. They were the Dawgs and getting so drunk that it showed was definitely not casual. Most of the time, they held their liquor well.

The sun was still a couple of hours from dipping into the ocean, and the afternoon breeze had mellowed to barely a whisper. Lunch had made up a bowl of guacamole, and he and two quite fit, sun-bleached, shaggy-haired young men were lounging in beach chairs, dipping Fritos and sipping bottles of Coors. Along with Dolphin and Lunch, Easy Ed Parks and Fast Eddie Hamilton made up the inner circle of the Surf Dawgs. As Lunch was twenty years older than everyone else, he didn't always join his younger brethren in all their radical exploits. Indeed, it wasn't necessary; he already had won his spurs. His former glory was such that he was more of an honorary Dawg—like a Nestor with the Greek warriors at Troy.

Lunch maneuvered a chip loaded with an inch-high pile of guacamole toward his mouth. Fast Eddie had just taken a pull on his beer, and Easy Ed had just "surf-snapped" a bottle cap in a contest to see who could snap their bottle caps the farthest. From up above, they heard somebody holler, "Incoming!" A body swung down from above, holding on to something like a bungee cord. Flying parallel to the pier, the body had to jackknife up to avoid hitting the Dawgs, and then swung past them and up almost to the height of the pier. On its circuit back, the body crashed into a hill of sand that shielded Lunch's camp from the Strand. When setting up his digs, Lunch had had his buddies who daily bulldozed the beach build up a sand wall to give him privacy and keep away the autograph hounds.

"Hi, Dolphin," Easy said, trying to be casual and not seem too impressed with his arrival.

"Hi, dawgs, Lunch," Dolphin said after he got his wind back, also shooting for casual.

"I'll give it an eight," said Fast, "for degree of difficulty and style, but not for execution."

"Nice of you to drop in," said Lunch, who though he didn't let on that he was startled, had nevertheless missed his mouth with the chip and now had a glob of guacamole enmeshed in his mustache.

"Next time," said Easy, "you need to use something other than surfboard leashes, though."

"Even three of them wound together was too flimsy," Dolphin shot back. "But I was in a hurry."

"Dude, Lunch was just telling us about his talk with you,"

Fast said. "You don't look like a dude who's been pullin' off the most un-casual, un-radical, behavior with a dudette in the Dawgs' history. Or is what Lunch's been telling just one of his stretchers?"

"You guys just don't understand women yet," Lunch said. "A fox like that can really mess a dude up." He took a swig of his beer. "Listen, Dolphin, I was rethinking how you should show interest in her. You know, that was the last thing you needed to do. No wonder you bombed. What I should have said was to treat her like she wasn't even there. Chicks love it. Neglect, Dawg, it works every time, especially with the utter foxes. They aren't used to it. When I told you that, it must have been right after Nicole chased me out of the house with my Hawaiian sling. Something like that will weird you out for a while."

"She chased you with a Hawaiian sling?" said Easy. Curled up next to Easy Ed was his yellow Labrador Retriever, named Easy Dog, who usually didn't move much or very fast. Even Easy Dog seemed to moan at the thought of being chased with a big metal spear that got propelled by a long elastic sling.

"It's true, she totally knocked me sideways," Dolphin said, "and it feels like there's no other girl in the world anymore. Well, that was then—but now," Dolphin gave the whoop the Dawgs mostly reserved for when they made awesome surf moves on really scary waves. "I mean I'm still totally slain, but I'm making progress, and I've got it under control."

"Well, that could just be the fastest one-eighty I've ever seen," said Lunch.

"Really, Dolphin, are you going to tell us what happened?" asked Fast, surf-snapping a bottle cap at him.

"It's all cool now," said Dolphin, getting up and doing a little dance.

Easy also picked up a cap and snapped it, and Lunch threw a chip at him.

Just then two T Beach policemen drove up to the camp on their ATVs.

"It would almost be worth getting a job if I got to drive one of those things around the beach," Fast said.

"They're Honda's new models, and they're awesome, like a light dune buggy," said Easy, who talked a lot about cars, even though he didn't have one.

"What do you think they want to talk to us about?" said Fast.

"Probably Dolphin's pier jump," said Easy.

"Don't sweat the small time, Sherlock," Lunch said getting up from his chair. "My camp down here isn't exactly permitted either."

After getting off their four-wheelers, the two officers strolled toward the Dawgs but stopped a respectful distance from the camp. The removal of their helmets revealed two heads of hair similar to the Dawg's but shorter.

"Hey, Donny and Phil, good to see you, man," Lunch said, "but can't you see I'm in the middle of something."

"Sorry, Lunch," said Donny, the taller of the two, "but we got to at least look like were checking it out. There was a report of somebody bungee jumping from the pier, and old man Richter was in dispatch."

"You should have seen it, dude, it was awesome," Lunch said. "Remember when we used to have the rope swing on the old Portuguese Bend pier, it was like that, but instead of landing in water, he crashed into that hill of sand, like Tarzan hitting a tree."

"I used to love going down there," said Donny.

"Portuguese Bend pier—that was a blast," said the other officer.

"Listen, we're in the middle of something now, come back later and I'll save you some guac, and if old man Richter has a problem, tell him to talk with me about it."

"All right, man, we got it," said Donny. "Be cool." The officers donned their helmets, went back to their vehicles, waved a cool little surfer's wave, and cruised off.

Lunch sat back down with an air of extreme self-contented casualness.

The three other Dawgs just looked at each other, stoked.

"Okay, Dolphin," said Easy, handing him a beer, "lay it on us, dude."

"Okay, here's the deal. It's true the date didn't go that great, especially at first. I was still spazzing out about half the time."

"You're all jazzed about only choking *half* the time?" said Easy.

"Well, I *am* going out with her again. She wants me to take her to a fancy dinner theater in Westwood."

"How you going to that?" said Fast.

"Dude, that's what I'm here to talk about, man. My moolah troubles are on the wane."

"You didn't get a job, did you?" Easy asked, concerned and comforting Easy Dog, who looked concerned as well.

"No, dawg, I got an idea!"

CHAPTER 7

Dolphin proceeded to talk about how Aunt Clemmie took off to New York for the summer and told him not to use the house for any of his ill-advised schemes. And that got him thinking, but the lightning didn't strike till he was walking down the Strand and saw a For Rent sign. Then, it all flashed on him—he would rent out the Sandcastle while Aunt Clemmie was away for the summer.

There was a moment of silence as the grandeur of the concept sunk in.

"Dude!" Easy Ed said breaking the silence.

"Awesome," said Fast Eddy, leaving off being totally casual.

"That is totally bitchin'," said Lunch, rubbing his hands together.

"Dawgs," said Dolphin, "an opportunity like this doesn't just happen every day. We have to do it right."

"It's like a big south swell coming during Christmas vacation," said Easy.

"It's more like one of the one-in-a-century swells, like the one that caused the *Dominator* to go down," said Lunch.

Fast Eddie cut him off, fearing a long story about an old freighter that split up on the rocks at Lunada Bay Point during a big swell in the winter of 1961. "I agree, dawg, it's true there might not be an opportunity like this in a long time. If you do it right, the beach will be talking about it for years."

"Yeah, we gotta be styling on it," Dolphin said, trying again to imitate what he thought was a Shakespearean word trick.

"Most definitely," said Fast.

"Most awesomely," said Easy.

"Delightful," Lunch said, and started rubbing his hands together again.

"Okay, dawgs," Dolphin said, "this is what I'm thinking. Instead of renting the whole place to one renter, we'll rent four of the bedrooms out separately, like a hotel, and we'll provide meals."

"That's good," said Lunch. "Way better return than renting the whole house. I spent a couple of winters on the North Shore at the Vanderloof mansion, and they rented it out like that."

"Maybe a couple of the rooms could go to chicks," Easy said.

"And we could include free surf lessons," Fast added.

"But we have to maximize revenue," said Lunch. "And I'm having trouble with the one source I have."

"And don't forget this whole idea is to help me afford going out with the only chick I care about in the whole world."

Easy and Fast grudgingly agreed.

Dolphin said, "We're going to need to appeal to different clientele."

"Dude, awesome word," said Easy. "Like people with bucks."

"And those kinda people," said Dolphin, "expect good service, and like to have people to boss around."

"Dude, who are we going to get for them to boss around?" asked Easy.

A few moments of silence passed as they pondered the problem. Dolphin finally broke it, exclaiming, "Why, you guys can do it!" The whole thing was now taking wondrous shape in his mind.

There was another period of silence, the other Dawgs making the disappointing connection that rather than having people to boss around, they might have to get bossed around themselves.

Dolphin sought to address their fears: "It won't be that bad or anything, you'll be the 'the staff.'"

There was a sigh of relief. Being staff didn't sound too bad.

In the end, after considerable negotiations, the assignments agreed on would require almost no work at all. Dolphin would be the proprietor, host, and landlord. Fast Eddie would take care of parking cars and carrying luggage—the bellhop so to speak. Easy would be the butler. This job was a "style" idea; Dolphin figured a classy establishment like theirs ought to have a butler, like Aunt Clemmie had in one of her books. This was going to be the most challenging of the assignments. But they all liked the ring of it, and Easy, being a Dawg, didn't hair out on the idea, though his fitness for it was questionable. Fast could also give surf lessons in his free time for tips, if any of the renters were inclined. But not Easy, for that seemed beneath the high office of a butler. Easy convinced Fast to promise to split the tips if he got any.

They all agreed that they would need maids. From experience, they knew that it would be a disaster if any of them tried to make beds, do laundry, or clean dishes. Lunch volunteered his girlfriend, Nicole, and one of her friends for the job, seeing it as a way to get back in good with her. He said he could spin it as a fun adventure, and she would get paid for it too.

But that left Lunch. As he sat, the sun lowering into the sea behind him, he was trying his best not to feel left out.

"Now, what have we forgotten?" asked Dolphin.

Lunch kept his head down, looking at the empty guacamole bowl. After all, he was human and had feelings, despite being twenty years older than them.

"A cook, dude, we need a cook," said Fast Eddie.

"Dawg, you're right," said Easy. "Who do we know that can cook?"

The Dawgs thought it over. Easy and Fast's food preparation didn't go much beyond cereal and toast. Dolphin was a little more sophisticated, being able to heat things up in the microwave oven Aunt Clemmie recently bought. All three of the Dawgs looked at each other, then to Lunch.

"You used to work at Tony's on the pier, didn't you?" Dolphin asked.

Lunch just proudly blushed.

"Dude, we need you. Will you do it?"

"You're a perfect fit for it," said Fast.

"Dude, you're a natural," said Easy.

"You'll have an awesome budget," said Dolphin. "The price of the rent will include meals, like in a bed and breakfast. We stayed in a couple of those in the Lake District in England when Aunt Clemmie took me there."

"Like in those all-you-can-eat breakfast buffets?" Fast said.

"No, dude," said Dolphin, "nothing like those."

"If you really need me," Lunch said, "I'll go for it and won't let you dawgs down."

So, it was nearly settled.

Then Dolphin said, "But the cook needs to be a live-in cook. You're going to have to move in for the summer. That a problem?"

There was another moment of silence. Lunch didn't mind going over to the Sandcastle while the sun was up, but as much as he could, he made sure not to be found there at night. When it came to most things in this life, he was the most fearless, radical person the Dawgs knew. But the Sandcastle at night had a hold over him. He didn't like the old stories about it being haunted, which he had heard about since he was a little kid. Moving into the Sandcastle was asking a lot of him. But then again, living under the pier wasn't exactly the ideal situation either. And he had his brother Dawgs to think about. He knew the Dawgs looked up to him, and he had the responsibility of setting an example. "Okay, I'll do it," he said.

"Awesome," Dolphin said, and then to Fast Eddy, "Do you think you could get your sister to print up some rental flyers for us? She probably does that kind of thing all the time."

"Sure, I'll tell her she'd be doing you a favor."

"Tell her we need them as soon as possible, and we'll give her a commission on the rents."

"Shouldn't be a problem. Saturdays they work late, she's probably in the office right now. How many do we want?"

"Five hundred," said Lunch, obviously quite enthusiastic about the whole idea.

"A hundred should do," said Dolphin. "We at least ought to try to hold down the expenses."

So, they all had their responsibilities. Dolphin offered to split all the profits evenly among the Dawgs and Lunch, but they wouldn't think of it. They determined that Dolphin would get half, and the rest would be split among them. They figured they should be able to gross close to $20,000 for the summer. And that would fund for them, among other things, a surf trip to the Islands that coming winter.

Now all they had to do was find some high-rolling renters.

CHAPTER 8

The planning meeting under the pier had been on Saturday; by Tuesday noon the plan was in full swing. Fast Eddie's twin sister, Emily, who worked as a secretary in a real estate office, had delivered the flyers to her brother the previous Sunday night. She'd been sweet on Dolphin off and on for years, so it was relatively simple to enlist her help, especially with the 3 percent commission they offered her. She designed the flyers from professional-looking examples from her office. For her commission she would also run an ad in the *T Beach Weekly* and handle interviewing and signing up the renters. For the flyers and ad, she named the property the Maison de Beach. The Dawgs dug it. By Monday noon the Dawgs had covered the Strand with flyers advertising "Exclusive Beach Front Rooms for Rent."

When Dolphin came back from lunch at Surf Burgers that Tuesday, passing through the front gate of the "Maison," he saw a girl sitting on the front doorstep, her head drooped over her knees, and bobbing up and down like she was having a mild paroxysm. When she looked up, having heard the gate open, he saw it was Claudette.

"Hey, cool, you're here," he said, walking up to her, feeling casual. He thought she might be doing some new form of yoga but figured it would be okay to interrupt her anyway.

She looked up at him, smeared tears trailed down her cheeks. "I de-de-deceived you," she sobbed.

Dolphin had been in a good mood. The thought of being offended didn't cross his mind.

"I deceived you," she splattered, this time, a little wetter than the first.

Dolphin subscribed to the ancient philosophy that all is fair in love and war. He wasn't a grudge-holding kind of guy anyway, and he did hate to see that face smeared with tears.

Dolphin said, "It's cool, don't worry. I kinda did the same to you. But it's going to be okay now. Please don't cry."

"When you said your name was Smoote with an "e" and you lived at the Beach in Tranquility, I knew you had to be related to Clementine Hardin," she said through her tears. "I've read so much about her. I've even read about your house," she said, calming a little.

"Aunt Clemmie's house," corrected Dolphin.

"But I was desperate."

"You were?"

"I lost my job."

"Your modeling job?"

"I punched some guy who gave me a funny look."

"I hope I don't look at you funny."

"He also said I waddled. Do I waddle?"

"Absolutely not. You sway a little which is really cool."

"You see, I'm broke. I needed the money."

"What did you do, pinch one of Aunt Clemmie's silver butter knives?"

"No. The book!" The tears started to flow again.

"It's okay, she's got plenty of books. I'm broke too. Or was. I mean I'm almost not."

"I didn't steal the book. When I knew I was coming down here, I bought a first edition with the last of my savings, thinking that if I could get it signed, it would be worth three times as much. But your aunt caught me."

"She's caught me for almost everything I've ever done too."

"Instead of signing as she normally does, she must have signed it left-handed. I took it to three different used book dealers. They all said it was a forgery and the first edition wasn't even worth what I paid for it originally."

"She *is* left-handed. She must have signed it with her right."

"I'm left-handed too."

"She is tricky. She says it's in her blood. Was the rest of your story true?"

"Yes, it's all true. I called my grandmother back in Oklahoma. She came clean with me. It's all true. I come from a long line of criminals. Maybe I'm nothing more than a criminal at heart."

"No more than I am. And it's what's going to make you a great writer, like Aunt Clemmie."

"Do you really think so?"

"Yep."

"But now I'm destitute."

"You mean you're broke?"

"Yes."

"Listen. I'm going to be coming into beaucoup moolah, soon, and I can help you out till you get on your feet again."

"I'll work, but I hate modeling."

At the beginning of this chapter, we described our hero as

being in a rather sunny mood where everything was chipper and looked like smooth sailing ahead. And actually, everything did look that way except for one large, lingering doubt floating around in his mind. That doubt was about Easy Ed's ability to do the important and difficult job of butler at the Maison de Beach. Now, another idea came to Dolphin.

"Do you know anything about butlering?" he asked.

"Why?"

"Well, I told you that I was having my own difficulties with the green stuff, but things were on the mend. Well . . ."—and here, after he got her to promise she would be zipper-lipped about it all, he told her the plan.

"And it's all good and tight—except I don't feel great about Easy's fit for butlerhood," he said. "Easy can be a little . . . volatile, I think's the word, at times."

"Will he listen to me? I could tell him what to do."

"He's kind of tightly wound—he's been known to go "ninja" on occasion."

"That could be a problem."

"And he doesn't have that—that certain butler quality."

"Gravitas?"

"Yeah. But maybe you could be the concierge, you know, like they have at fancy hotels. Those are sometimes females."

"No, no, I could be the butler—I played Jeeves in a high school play."

"Who?"

"This famous, very proper and dignified British gentleman's gentleman," she said, in a very proper and dignified tone and posture. "That's what they call butlers in England."

"You mean you would dress up like a . . ."

"I did it in the play, and I got good reviews. I'm tall and can get a wig and tuck my hair in and talk with a deep voice." Here she gave a few examples, which were fairly good.

As we have seen, the Dawgs are very conscientious about "style," and the opportunity for the style of this was just too overwhelming to resist.

"If you could really pull it off, that would be so gnarly!" Dolphin said, using a word he saved for only the most illustrious occasions. "That would be totally gnarly." Then he checked himself, not wanting to be too forward or too suggestive. "But the butler will need to be here most of the time. We were planning on Easy moving into the extra room downstairs, where my aunt's assistant stays."

"Actually, it wouldn't be too much trouble. If Easy could stay someplace else, I could stay in that room—you see, I am a bit short on rent this month"

"Sure, Easy and Fast can share a room."

"We would get to spend a lot of time together," she said.

"I would like that—a lot," he said.

"I would like that a lot too."

CHAPTER 9

Just about the same time that Tuesday afternoon, a mile and a half to the south of the Maison, *Borrowed Time*, a forty-three-foot sailboat limped into the dock at the Safe Haven Harbor Yacht Club. The yacht club and its facilities included a couple of outdoor tennis courts, three indoor squash courts, a small workout room, a bar with a small restaurant, and a dry dock with a yacht-repair facility, but had no overnight boarding. *Borrowed Time*'s captain was much chagrined when told—after the inspection of the boat's hull, and the manager of the facility had made a number of phone calls—that it would take up to ten weeks to get the parts and refit a sizable section of the lower bow.

After signing some paperwork and paying a deposit in cash, the captain of the boat said, "If there's any way you can speed things up, I will make it more than worth your while."

"It's the parts, man—can't do much without the parts."

"Well, this is going to be a problem," the captain said. He had short salt-and-pepper hair and a cowboy mustache, the sides of which drooped down toward his chin. He was quite fit for his middle age, and *Semper fi* was tattooed on his left forearm. "I'm going to need to find me a place where I can get my equipment set up, a private and quiet place, with a good view of the southern sky."

"Hmm," said the manager of the boat yard, apparently pondering the statement, "Hmm."

"I'll be in a hurry to find me a place," he reiterated. "Ya know, time is money."

"You aren't from around, are you?" the manager of the yard said, rubbing his chin and manifesting good beach casualness by not being in much of a hurry himself.

"Originally from Texas, sir, but I've been around a bit. If you have any ideas, I'd be thankful."

"Well, something like that isn't going to be easy to find, except maybe up on the Strand you might find something, but that's not going to be cheap. Possible the receptionist up in the club might be able to help you out."

"I'm obliged," the boat owner said, handing the manager a fifty-dollar bill. "And I'd appreciate it if you keep an eye on my rig till I get back and can get my things. And let me know if anyone comes snooping around. Got some valuable equipment in there."

Three hours later, a dark blue sedan with three persons in it—a woman and two men—drove up to the yacht club.

"Now, keep to the plan," the woman, who had been driving, said as they exited the car. "You know your rolls, and even in here we play by them. We don't want to spook him."

"Roger that," said that man who had been in the back seat. He was tall, in his midthirties, with short-cropped hair "white-walled" on the sides, and his pencil mustache closely trimmed.

"Don't worry, Cloris, my part's easy. I got it under control." He was short and plump with a comb-over partially covering his male-pattern baldness.

They got out of the car and, bypassing the yacht club office, proceeded to the dry dock. Through the fence closing off the area from the rest of the facility, they saw what they were looking for. But the gate was locked, and though the younger man of the party was tempted to jump the fence, he didn't.

They didn't get to talk to the manager of the repair facility until the next morning. But they did talk to the receptionist in the yacht club office. She, too, had received a fifty-dollar bill from the captain of *Borrowed Time*. And though she didn't say much, she did mention that the nice gentleman who owned the boat seemed to be interested in a place to stay up on the beach.

CHAPTER 10

Just a mile up the Strand, right across the border where Tranquility Beach ends and Manhattan Beach begins, another scene involving two people of the opposite sex was taking place. A lanky young man with a mullet haircut had been checking if there was any surf worth marring that afternoon down toward T Beach. Determining it wasn't worth going out, he started on his skateboard back up the bike path. Alex Cutter—or Tree, as Crazy Ahab and the other Village Idiots called him—was cruising at a good clip as he passed an interesting-looking young female in an interesting-looking bathing suit. His interest must have been considerable, because he kept looking at her after he had passed by, until he heard in a rather strained, high-pitched tone, "On your right!"

The voice was from one of those altogether too common types who think they own the bike path: a cyclist. This particular bike rider was decked out to resemble something out of the Tour de France, though not necessarily as trim as most of those riders. If Tree had had the time to be philosophical about it, he might have speculated on the contrast between the young lady he had just been eyeing, and one on the bicycle who was about to splatter him onto the pavement. But Tree only had a second to determine which direction was his right. Before he could solve the puzzle, the bike and rider were upon him.

The cyclist did an admirable job of swerving, so her bicycle only barely grazed him. What did hit him squarely was her large, outstretched arm, which she had flung out trying to push him away. Missing his shoulder, she clotheslined him, as they call it in football, catching Tree squarely in the Adam's apple with her forearm. The cyclist rode on a few feet before stopping to look back, and Tree collided face-first into a garbage can along the wall of the bike path.

"Asshole!" she yelled back with some vigor. "Why don't you look where you're going!"

As it was apparent that the skateboarder with the strange haircut had gotten the worst of it, the lady rode off in disgust. Tree was only slightly fazed from the incident physically, and not at all emotionally. He was not unused to taking his lumps. His Adam's apple, large and sturdy, didn't hurt too much, although when he would try to speak later, he would notice a new timbre to his voice. He hit the garbage can largely with his forehead, which was, luckily, well-padded with bone. He could live with a bump. And even if the bump got big, his long bangs could hide it. And as far as the ol' inner child went, he'd been called the name she'd yelled at him so many times before that he didn't even notice. Thankfully, he could keep the affair just between him and the garbage can, which was a relief. He knew that if Crazy Ahab or any of the other Idiots heard about it, they would not be kind.

Even in the worst happenings, something positive can usually be found. And as Tree was sitting on the path, rubbing his head and staring at the silver gleam of the garbage can, he saw something that grabbed his attention. On the side of the can was a flyer with a picture of a familiar house. At first, he thought perhaps it was advertising a keg party. But he began to doubt this theory when he saw the words, "For Summer Rental." After a few moments of staring, it flashed on him that this was none other than the house where Dolphin Smoote lived, the Village Idiots' bitter enemy. And if there was one thing the Idiots didn't care for (and there were many) it was beach residents who rented their places out to tourists and foreigners. Tree decided Ahab and the rest of the Idiots needed to see this.

After stopping at a restroom along the bike path to tidy up, Tree found one of the other Idiots a mile up the beach. JD Pitts—who liked to be called Howl, from the title of a book of poetry he had never read—was out on the beach, scanning the sand with a device that looked something like a weed whacker but was, in fact, a metal detector. And it looked like he had found something.

By the time Tree walked out to the site of inspection, Howl, having put down his detector, was digging intently in the sand. "Dude, where'd you get this?" Tree asked, picking up the detector. Howl hadn't bothered to take off his earphones, by which the detector communicated its signals through a six-foot cord. Howl neither heard nor saw Tree. He did, however, feel the earphones jerk his head back when Tree started swinging the detector around and pointing it to the sky, pretending it was an antiaircraft gun shooting down planes.

Howl ripped the earphones off and, turning, saw Tree. "Dude," he yelled, "what are you doing, trying to break my neck?"

"Sorry, man. Where'd you get this?" Tree asked again, holding up the metal detector.

"My old man gave it to me. He got it from one of his

clients," said Howl. "It took him two and a half years, but the wife ended up with almost everything, even her husband's metal detector. She didn't want it."

"If I ever get divorced, I'm going to hire your old man."

"You couldn't afford him. Now clamp it and help me look," he said, and went back to his digging.

Tree put the metal detector down and started digging too. "What are we digging for?"

"I don't know, but the thing started going crazy. They had a big volleyball tournament down here Sunday. Maybe somebody lost something valuable."

As Tree was digging, a tinny beeping sound came seeping out of the sand a few feet away.

Tree, moving more quickly than Howl, went to the spot in the sand where the beeping was coming from and dug. Under about four inches of sand, he uncovered a pager.

"Dude, this is your pager, isn't it?"

Howl immediately patted the pocket of his board shorts but didn't find what he was looking for. "Give it to me," he demanded.

Tree stepped a few feet away and started reading out loud the message on its display: "Darling, it's a warm day, don't overheat—"

Howl had wrestled it out of his hand.

"Dude," said Tree laughing and hiccuping at the same time. You thought you found some big treasure, but it was only your own pager. That's like something some honky Val would do. And then mommy pings you to save the day, man. Wait till Crazy Ahab hears about this."

"He better not, beanpole. If he does, I'll tell him about you crashing on the bike path again."

"How do you know about that?" said Tree, turning serious.

"The blood dripping down your knee was a start. I heard some people on the Strand talking about some punk on a skateboard who crashed into a garbage can. I figured it had to be you."

"If you won't tell, I won't tell," Tree said.

"Alright," said Howl. He was about a head shorter than Tree, a bit plump, wore glasses, and his shoulder-length hair was already thinning. "Or I won't let you sleep in my garage anymore."

"I won't, but don't you think we ought to tell Crazy Ahab about *this*?" He took the flyer advertising the Sandcastle for rent from his pocket. "Scope it out, dude. Smoote's renting out the Sandcastle! His aunt must be gone. She would never rent the place out."

There was a moment of thoughtful silence. "That's not the real issue, slush brain," said Howl, after studying the flyer for twenty seconds. "It's that he's bringing in nonlocals to the beach. He's encouraging the invasion."

Howl looked at the flyer again. "You're right," he said. "Ahab needs to see this."

It took JD and Tree twenty minutes to journey up past Manhattan Beach to where Sea Urchin Lane ended at the bike path. After turning onto the lane, and going up a block and a half, they came to the abode of Wolfgang Schenck Junior, or Crazy Ahab, as he was more commonly known. His parents, both child psychologists, had purchased the California bungalow as an investment and let him live there rent free, not fully applying the counsel they would give to others in similar situations. But as comfortable as the place was, Ahab resented the indignity of living a block and a half down a side street and not directly on the Strand. He wasn't shy about letting his parents know about it either.

"Hey, slime buckets." Crazy Ahab said to Howl and Tree when they entered the house. He wore a pith helmet with mosquito netting that draped down from its perimeter, covering his face. With a roll of duct tape, he was sealing the edges of the windows in his living room.

"Dude, why are you taping up your windows?" asked Tree.

"Yellow jackets, man, I'm being invaded by yellow jackets. Somehow, they're getting in, I think it's through the sides of these windows," he said, and lifted his mosquito netting, showing five or six sizable welts on his cheeks and chin.

"We had 'em once, and my mom's boyfriend fried out their nest," Tree offered. "He sprayed a can of hairspray at it and then lit it on fire. Man, it was awesome, the whole thing blazed up and the bugs just melted, dude, and didn't come back. Earl did get stung about ten times, but it was worth it."

"That's bad karma, man, messing with the ecosystem," said Crazy Ahab. In reality, the house and yard just had a bad case of sand fleas. He had heard somewhere that yellow jackets fed on them, so, he had ordered three nests of the wasps from the local pet store and set them up outside in his yard. As karma would have it, they had now found a way into his house.

The heart of the problem was not the yellow jackets, however. Though his parents let him stay in the house for free, he was supposed to be responsible for maintenance and utilities. His parents did try to hold to this policy, but for Ahab it was an unacceptable burden to bear. In a moment of magnanimity, he thought he might try to get rid of the yellow jackets before he demanded the rights of a renter and made his parents fumigate the house for fleas.

"Are there many of them left in here now?" asked Howl. "I don't want to get stung."

"Just a few. I've killed about twenty of them with a flip-flop. They take a few hours to regroup and reattack. I have some extra mosquito net you can drape over your face if you want."

"I do, man," said Howl. "I could be allergic to them."

"Me too," said Tree, who didn't like being left out.

Unfortunately, there was only enough netting to cover Howl. He rigged up something with a baseball cap which gave off the appearance of a woman's hat from the 1940s that was worn at funerals. Fortunately for Tree, Crazy Ahab's parents had stocked the kitchen with utensils, and in there he found a large colander. He strapped this over his face, so only the back of his head was unprotected. This gave him a slight resemblance to a villain in a low-budget horror movie.

After Tree had secured his protection, Howl handed Ahab the flyer. Deciphering the subtext of the flyer had taken Tree some time, possibly because he had just crashed headfirst into a garbage can. It had taken Howl a little study as well, as his glasses were fogged up from overheating himself while digging for treasure. But it only took Crazy Ahab a few seconds, even through his mosquito netting. He immediately tore up the flyer and flung it to the floor.

"We ain't taking this lying down," Ahab said, throwing off his pith helmet. "There's just so much I can take, especially after what he did to us last month." A yellow jacket landed on his arm. With his bare hand he whacked it, squishing the bug.

CHAPTER 11

Though time's scythe was hacking away in the "rest of the world"—what the Dawgs called most anywhere else—it had left Tranquility Beach relatively unscathed. T Beach was still an enclave of the sleepy, slow, and mostly quiet earlier Southern California beach culture. The Dawgs and other true surfers thrived in this atmosphere, adding a touch of casual radicalness to it, and thus defining a lifestyle. The quiet and peace was also the reason Aunt Clemmie kept her residence there—it was an ideal setting for her to write. It is questionable if it was an ideal place for Dolphin's entrepreneurial venture.

It was the Wednesday after the Dawg's meeting under the pier, and Fast Eddie's sister, Emily, received her first response from her flyers. The man who had called said, in a southern drawl, that he had seen the flyer and was very interested. He needed a place to stay while his boat had repairs made. As the flyer had included the address, he had already passed by and reconned (the word he used) the Maison de Beach, and the place looked ideal. He especially liked the looks of that top-floor apartment with the balcony.

"Oh, you mean the Eagle's Nest," Emily said, coming up with that embellishment on the spot. On the top floor, all by itself, nice and private, spacious with a wonderful view."

"Nice and private with a good view?"

"Yes, almost a hundred-and-eighty-degree view."

"That sounds perfect, just what I'm looking for."

"Of course, it's a little more expensive than the other rooms."

"That's not going to be a problem. But before I layout three months in advance, I'd like to take a look this afternoon."

This was going faster than the plans had called for. Bringing him by the house on such short notice could be a disaster. "If you come by my office tomorrow," she stalled, "you can fill out a rental application. We'll need that filled out first, and on approval, a deposit."

"Yes, I'll do that, but before I pay up, I would like to take a gander, especially like to see the view from up there."

This was reasonable, particularly as price didn't seem to be an issue for him. But she had to put him off for at least a day. "It might be possible for you to see the property tomorrow afternoon, after you fill out the application. The current patrons are checking out tomorrow and guest services will need time to service the rooms."

"Well, if that's the best you can do, I'll have to hole up at my hotel another night," he said.

"So sorry to inconvenience you, sir."

"That's nice of you, ma'am. If you could give me your office address, I'll swing right by and pick up an application."

"Oh, yes, we're in the suite above the comedy club, one block south of the pier."

After the call, Emily immediately called Dolphin and told

him the good news of their first perspective renter. Dolphin was "stoked," which in surfer argot means *excited*. He in turn immediately found Claudette, who was in the Maison den writing up some lists. When she heard the news, she panicked.

It was almost two more hours before Fast Eddy and Easy Ed finally arrived back at the Maison for the "all hands" meeting Claudette had immediately called after getting the news from Dolphin. They had been up the beach, watching a volleyball tournament. "Did you see Dolphin?" she asked, "I sent him looking for you and Lunch." She was holding a couple of pieces of paper and walking around in circles. "We have less than twenty-four hours to get this place up and running, and we're not even close to being ready." There was definitely something un-casual in her voice.

"What else do we need to do?" asked Easy. "The house looks clean. All the beds are made."

"What else? Everything!" Claudette said. "You and Fast don't have uniforms and badges, Lunch hasn't gone shopping. Where is he? And where's Dolphin? I don't have my butler's uniform yet, and I can't show the room until I have my uniform. And, we don't have any money yet."

Just then, Dolphin and Lunch walked in. Dolphin sporting a shy grin and carrying a bouquet of flowers.

"Oh, flowers for the house, that's at least a good idea," she said. "But we have so much more to do."

Dolphin's grin melted.

"I did put together the lists you told me to," said Lunch, handing her three sheets of paper.

She took a glance at his lists. "There's enough here to feed the Kansas City Chiefs," she said. Her roots being in Kansas, the Chiefs were her favorite team.

"Okay, let's be cool," said Dolphin. "Everything is going to be fine. I talked to Emily again, and she's going to put the renter off till five p.m. tomorrow to see the room and Friday to move in. So, we have the rest of today and most of the day tomorrow to get ready for his checking it out. Then if he likes it, he's agreed to pay in advance. So, we'll have some money and a whole day to get everything ready. The house is in pretty good shape, but we'll go over it again and make sure it's perfect before this guy comes to check it out. And Emily will be the one who shows him the house, and none of us will need to be around."

"Emily!" Claudette interrupted. She wasn't fond of Emily.

"Yes, you won't have your uniform yet, so you can't do it. She says he's already filled out his application, and it looks good great. She checked his credit rating and it's like eight hundred something. She says that's really good. And he wants Aunt Clemmie's room with her balcony and he's willing to pay in advance, once he sees the room. He's paying fifty percent more. He wanted to see the place today, but she put him off till late tomorrow. And she's going to tell him that a new air conditioner is getting installed and he won't be able to move in till Friday. So, if he goes for it, we'll have more than enough money to buy everything we need, and a whole day to shop and get ready. But all of you need to move in tomorrow morning."

"That sounds like it could work," Claudette said. "How much is she charging us for this?"

"I offered her three percent."

"Three percent! She's taking us to the cleaners."

Dolphin handed the flowers to Claudette. "Well, Bertram—if that's what you are going to call yourself—now what?"

Emily's showing of the Maison went well, to say the least. The prospective renter, an apparently rich middle-aged Texan, raved about the view of the southern sky from the balcony of his room-to-be. "This'll be just right for the bit of equipment I need to set up," he had said. "The device isn't that big, and it don't use much power. I could throw in a little extra for it, if that is needed."

Emily told him the premium for his room would be sufficient. When she brought up the payment, he asked if cash would be a problem. She said it would be just fine. As soon the Texan took off, Emily sought out Dolphin and delivered the cash, minus her 3 percent.

"Piece of cake," said Emily. "I'm meeting a few more interested folks tomorrow morning in my office."

"They seem interested?" This was going even better than Dolphin had hoped.

"Totally! All three of them called, one right after the other. But I'll check them out in person. When I told them the rooms were going fast and a rich Texan had already nabbed the top floor, they all wanted to move in as soon as possible."

"They didn't even want to see the place?" Dolphin asked.

"They said they went by it and it looked great. I'll give you a call and let you know how it goes. Ciao," said Emily, as she walked out.

And she did call him the next day. She told him she had

signed up and received payment for three more renters, who had paid by check. They would be moving in on Saturday.

And so, the Dawgs—Claudette now was considered one of the tribe—had their renters, or patrons, as Claudette insisted they were to be called. The Texan, whose name was Mr. William Wiley, was something of an itinerant sailor, sailing around alone in the sunny climes in a forty-three-foot sailboat that he had rigged to sail by himself. The hull of his boat had started taking on serious water near the Isthmus of Catalina Island, twenty-five miles off the coast of Southern California. From there, he had managed to slow down the leak long enough to get his boat towed into the Safe Harbor Marina. He was going to be landlocked for a good ten weeks, so a nice, quiet, peaceful rental close by was exactly what he needed. He said he was a former security consultant and now just did a little investing, mostly when it was quiet and peaceful late at night. He made it clear that privacy and quiet were of utmost importance to him.

A woman and two men formed the rest of the patrons. If she could have managed it, Emily would have preferred three men. She always thought it better to have fewer females around. Though she wasn't exactly chasing Dolphin anymore, she did see this whole "Maison" situation as an opportunity to impress him, which might be of some use in the future. By her calculation, the female patron was a bit frumpy and wouldn't be getting much attention anyhow.

Her name was Ms. Cloris Root. She wore her hair pulled back like an onion, glasses with dark heavy rims, and a muumuu. She was probably in her late thirties. The way she asked about the rich Texan who had the top floor made Emily think she was looking for a husband. She said she was from Texas too and had a law practice back home.

The last two renters were a Mr. Marshall Mallow, a semi-retired tax lawyer from Phoenix, and a Sergeant Gerald Snipe, newly discharged from the Marines and, after the summer, on his way to Stanford Business School. They, too, showed some interest in the fellow who had rented the room on the top floor. Only Mr. Mallow seemed concerned about the price.

By late Saturday, the four renters had moved in with little fuss or difficulty, except for the complaints of Fast Eddie, on whom the brunt of the work fell. Being the bellhop, he was made to carry Mr. Wiley's equipment up to Aunt Clemmie's room on the fourth floor. The sizable tip he received helped him recover from the experience.

CHAPTER 12

The first few weeks of business at the Maison de Beach were relatively uneventful. Other than at meals, the patrons largely kept to themselves. A sizable south swell hit the beaches, and the Dawgs, especially Easy and Fast, spent as much time as they could out in the water. Claudette thought this was better than having them hanging around and getting in the way. Dolphin stayed around the house more, trying to be helpful where he could, unless the waves got really good. She told him he was adapting well to the role of landlord and host, and when he was around, she waited on him almost as much as she did the patrons. She kept her hair tucked up into a suitable wig, and attired herself in a black suit, pressed white shirt, and black bow tie, now in full butler mode.

Surfing wasn't Dolphin's top priority anymore. Nor was his role as proprietor of the house. Claudette was. He was nuts about her. And though he wasn't acting like a total moron anymore, it appeared to him he wasn't making much progress. At least that was the situation from Dolphin's perspective. But love is blind, as they say, and there are other perspective's worth considering—in this case, Claudette's.

Claudette was managing the day-to-day activities of the Maison, running nearly the whole concern on Dolphin's behalf. She even got him a bank account with his own checks. She was keeping his insane friends in line, flattering him daily, telling him what a great job he was doing. What else she could possibly do to show the imbecile how she felt about him? And how was he responding? He didn't seem to notice. He really wasn't half the idiot he let on to be, but when was he going to do something? She wanted her man to sweep her off her feet, to woo her with protestations of being unable to breathe without her, to slay dragons for her, to rescue her from scimitar-wielding Saracens.

But Dolphin was, above all else, casual—too casual perhaps. Claudette had thought his feelings for her were like her own for him, but now she didn't know. She finally decided to have a talk with that voice of authority and well of experience, Lunch Biggunes.

She found Lunch in his room, resting before he had to start cooking dinner. Actually, he was asleep, a mild roar with the decibel rating of a minor earthquake coming from his sinuses. She apparently didn't notice he was sleeping, or didn't care, because she barged into the room, the tears beginning to flow, saying, "Oh, Lunch, I am so unhappy."

It took Lunch a few moments to sort out why a dude in a black suit was running into his room, crying like a girl. But Lunch soon shook out the cobwebs and realized it was Bertram the butler crying like a girl. Then he recalled that Bertram *was* a girl.

"Why are you crying, Bertram—I mean, Claudette?" Lunch asked. He was truly a tender soul underneath the crust.

"I don't know what to do. I've tried everything, and he still doesn't like me?"

"Who doesn't like you?"

"Dolphin!" Claudette exclaimed.

"Are you nuts? He's crazy about you. He's so crazy about you it took him three weeks before he could say anything to you without gagging."

"That was then."

"He's so crazy about you he only goes surfing when the waves are really good."

"Well, why doesn't he show it?"

"He's trying to show it."

"He doesn't try very hard."

"That's just his style. He's a Surf Dawg."

"A what?"

"He's a real casual dude."

"I've tried everything to show him how much I care."

"Wait a minute." Lunch was pretty much fully awake now. "Are you telling me you like him, like, you know, you *like* like him?"

"That's what I've been telling you the last five minutes."

"He thinks you like his aunt more than you like him."

"I admire her, but I'm crazy about him."

"This is awesome. He's going to be stoked. All I have to do is tell him."

"You can't."

"Why?"

"Because it's not my style."

"Oh, style pile. There's a time for style and there's a time not for style. Style usually gets in the way of love."

"I came here so you could tell me what to do."

"Well, first of all, don't cry anymore. You've been doing great as the butler, and if the renters see you with puffy eyes, they'll think something's fishy." She had already pretty much stopped crying; this was just so she wouldn't start again.

"Second of all, you have to realize he does like you. He's nuts about you."

"Then why doesn't he show it?"

"It's just a thing with the younger dudes these days. They take this casual thing way too far. In my day, dude, when we liked a chick, we'd do anything." Of course, here Lunch was just blowing gas. He didn't know what else to say. "Let me think about it for a minute," he added after a few moments.

"I already tried not paying attention to him, pretending he's not even there. That wasn't very easy, and it didn't work very well. Though I guess he did ask me out."

"You did that?"

"And then I tried showing interest in him and his friends."

"Didn't work, did it?"

"I've been doing all the work, running the Maison, and letting him take credit for it."

"Don't stop doing that. If you weren't running the house, this whole thing would crash and burn."

"What should I do then?"

"I'm afraid," said Lunch, with a look of resolve filling his face, "it's going to call for drastic measures."

"Oh, no." She almost started to cry again.

"Don't worry," Lunch said. "Just leave it to me."

CHAPTER 13

As noted, in Dolphin's relationship with Claudette, more than one perspective existed. And often there are more than two—in this there were also Fast's and Easy's. Dawgs are always desirous to help each other out when one of them is in a jam, and they didn't like seeing their leader still not himself. Their motives, however, were not altogether altruistic. Animating them was also a certain amount of irritation toward Claudette. They were tired of getting bossed around. It wasn't that they didn't like her, she was just not at all causal about everything. She hadn't been in SoCal long enough to allow the sun and surf to mellow her out. So, desiring to be efficient in their expenditure of energy, they figured out how they could both help their friend and have some fun with Claudette at the same time.

It was Fast Eddy who came up with the initial idea, and then they both tweaked it with certain stylistic elements. What the situation called for was the Green Monster, though they wouldn't have known it by that term. They would help Dolphin's wooing of Claudette by bringing another girl into the picture and making her jealous.

"All the chick would have to do is to come up to Dolphin while Claudette's around and flirt around and say goofy stuff to him," Fast said.

"Like what?" asked Easy.

"She could just pretend like she's whispering in his ear, then she wouldn't have to be saying anything," said Fast. "That drives chicks crazy when they don't know what another chick is saying."

"Drives me crazy too," said Easy. "But who we gonna get to do it?"

"How about your sister, Emily?" suggested Easy. "Dude, remember when they got their braces stuck together playing spin the bottle in fifth grade?"

"Dude, it took us ten minutes to get them apart," said Fast, still not comfortable with that episode. "I don't believe they were really stuck, anyway. Dolphin just didn't want to let go."

"She'd be awesome," said Easy. "She did a great job signing up the renters."

"The problem would be getting her not to go overboard," her brother said.

In the meantime, Lunch was also at work trying to come up with a plan to help Claudette. Thinking that getting Nicole involved would help him get back into her good graces, he decided to solicit her help. They came up with the idea that he, being the cook and all, could put on a Maison de Beach barbeque. Nicole would be his assistant.

"This is totally tight, Sweet Pea," Lunch said to Nicole, using the sobriquet he used for her when the sailing was smooth. "Now what?"

They were sitting on Lunch's bed in his room at the Maison. Nicole had a pad of paper on her lap, writing out her plan. Lunch was sitting close by, getting in position to maybe steal a kiss if the opportunity arose. "Oh, ducky"—for that is what she called him—"we're going to make this real juicy. How does this sound?" she asked, reading what she had written:

I'll make it known that I'm inviting a friend to the bar-beque to help me serve.

Claudette will come as my helper, dressed as herself and all dolled up.

Ducky to convince her it will work and she won't be recognized by renters.

Claudette makes Dolphin jealous by showing atten-tion to someone else.

Ducky will tell her all she needs to do is talk with this someone and dance with him a couple of dances.

Who should be Mr. Someone? One of the renters! The youngest one, the ex-marine, makes the most sense.

Ducky tells ex-marine that there's a chick coming to the barbeque who saw him on the beach and is interested.

Ducky tells him that the chick loves soldiers and wants to hear all about his stories. Ducky does not tell Claudette this part of the plan.

Ducky will put on some good dance music for them and tell ex-marine that he should show her some of his moves. Ducky won't tell Claudette this part of the plan.

Ducky tells ex-marine that during the third song, which will be a slow number, to dance real close to her. Ducky won't tell Claudette this part of the plan.

When this happens, Ducky urges Dolphin to be a man and demonstrate his love by breaking in on Claudette and ex-marine. Ducky definitely won't tell Claudette this part of the plan.

To Lunch there were a couple of significant flaws in the plan. One of which was he had to do the dirty work of getting Claudette to go for it. He was okay with almost everything else. Or at least, he didn't think anything in the plan was worth criticizing. Nicole didn't take criticism well. But there was still one thing that Lunch just couldn't let go. He was concerned with her choice for the executor of the plan—the ex-marine, Sergeant Snipe.

Lunch had to handle this delicately, for Nicole was an artist at heart. "That is totally awesome. I love it. It's perfect. You don't think, though, it's a little . . . you know, too much?"

"Not at all," said Nicole. "Do you think Claudette would sit on his lap if you asked her to?"

"It's Sergeant Snipe. He's a little . . . intense, Sweet Pea. He just got out of the Marines and was Special Forces or something. He's still a bit on edge. Some kid lit a firecracker on the beach the other day and he jumped into a survival stance, ready to pounce. It looked a little like Crazy Ahab's surfing stance—you know, with his legs spread about two feet wider than the shoulders, knees bent about sixty degrees, arms and hands outstretched. If Dolphin tries to separate them, Snipe might go ninja on him. Remember our goal is to make Dolphin jealous, not send him to the ER."

In the end, like on those rare occasions in female-male relationships, they worked a compromise. By Lunch agreeing to do all the dirty work, he got her to change her choice of jealousy agents. That was about as smooth as Lunch had been for a long time and showed how much he was missing Nicole.

The alternatives to Sergeant Snipe were limited. Nicole said using one of the other Dawgs would lack style. That left one of the other two male renters, Mr. Wiley or Mr. Mallow. It wasn't an easy choice. Both of them appeared to be north of forty. But Nicole pointed out that that wasn't an issue, as younger girls often went for older guys when they had money, like Fast Eddie's sister and her current forty-year-old squeeze. And both Mr. Mallow and Mr. Wiley appeared to have plenty. Nicole added, "But not me, Ducky, I love you even if you're broke." Lunch took this as a big compliment.

As mentioned, William Wiley was from Texas and had told the Dawgs he now spent most of his time sailing around in his boat. He appeared to be quite a unique fellow, and he liked to say that he needed his open spaces and that the only place where there weren't fences anymore was out at sea. He also said his sailboat was his horse, it just ate less. He said he was "a rambling cowpoke in a boat, because that was all that was left for his kind." By all appearances, he was loaded from what he made in his night trading. Nicole said he wasn't unattractive and that his mustache with dropping sides was cute.

The other option was Marshall Mallow. He was about the same age as Mr. Wiley, but his hair left something to be desired. He seemed to be proud of having been a tax lawyer and was able to retire early. Also somewhat eccentric, he didn't say very much until he got going, and then wouldn't stop. But when he wasn't talking, he tended to fall asleep, no matter where he was.

Nicole and Lunch agreed that Mr. Mallow's proclivities toward slumber wouldn't be a good thing, and Mr. Wiley wasn't such a bad choice. He was fit and self-confident, which could kind of make up for some of the age difference. And he appeared to be of an amorous disposition—he would regularly flirt with Nicole, the other maid, and most any other female biped that came along, with the exception of Ms. Root. The clincher, in Lunch's mind, was that he would be a minimal threat to Dolphin's life and limb when Dolphin, as they hoped, would save Claudette from his advances.

Nicole even ended up going with Lunch to get Claudette's sign-off on the plan; she wanted to make sure Lunch didn't screw it up. The point that convinced Claudette was when Lunch said, "Maybe Dolphin's lack of passion is related to seeing you in the last couple of weeks dressed only as a butler." Lunch reasoned, "It might be helpful if he was reminded you were a woman." This was difficult to disagree with, and Claudette came on board, though not without reservations.

When Fast and Easy heard about the party, they thought it would be the perfect place to execute their plan. For a brief moment, they thought their idea had fallen apart when they heard that Claudette wasn't coming to the party. But when they tried to talk her into coming, she assured them that she would be there, as a surprise, a little after things started. This, they figured, might even be better—when Claudette got there, Emily could already be hanging all over Dolphin. If Fast and Easy had taken the trouble not to ditch out on their high school psychology classes, and if Nicole had listened during hers, they would have known the importance of interpersonal communication and understood the need to coordinate their schemes.

Psychology was barely invented when Lunch was in school, so he had a valid excuse. It happened, therefore, that neither set of plotters had a clue what the other was doing. And of course, Dolphin didn't have a clue about anything. The barbeque was where both conspiracies would be executed. And Dolphin didn't know he was to be the executee.

CHAPTER 14

The day of the barbeque arrived. The surf was ripping, about eight-foot with even larger sets. The sky was a beautiful light blue. There was almost no wind, only a wispy cloud or two, no fog, and the smog was way worse in the Valley. The mercury lounged in the mideighties.

Now, stereotyping just doesn't work and is unfair. Just because Claudette had bank robbers and other crooks in her family line didn't mean she was without class and hadn't learned manners. The point is, she had a degree of sophistication and wanted to make sure all the patrons felt comfortable, got acquainted with one another, and enjoyed themselves at the party. Thus, she had given Lunch emphatic instructions on what to do and not do until she and Nicole arrived. A simple summary of those instructions was: "Try to make the patrons feel at home, and don't do anything else until Nicole and I get back."

As mentioned, the surf was hot, and even glassy past noon. Dolphin and the other Dawgs had gone to the breakwater, where it was peeling off perfect lefts. The party was set to start at 5:00 p.m., and Dolphin had told Lunch they'd be back by 3:00 p.m. But Lunch was eager to get going. By 12:51, just after he had finished his lunch chores, he began preparations. Out on the patio, where the barbeque would be held, he filled up two chests full of ice and microbrews. He rolled out Aunt Clemmie's mobile liquor cabinet, which was stocked with a variety of high-proof refreshments. And now, in a large cooler he mixed up a batch of what he was calling "Organic Mayhem." This putatively healthy concoction would be sure to loosen up the patrons considerably. At its base was 80 proof vodka and 151 proof rum, which was hardly noticeable amid the freshly blended guava, blueberry, and orange juices it was mixed with. After notching up the alcohol content with more rum, he found it was nearly perfect.

But Lunch hadn't arrived at his station in life without considering others. He figured that if the plan he had made with Nicole were going to work, precision was called for. The main participants would require clear heads and shouldn't be drinking alcohol. Lunch therefore made another batch without the vodka and rum. When he was finished, he taped labels on the two coolers, one saying "Organic Mayhem," the other "Virginic Delight." Lunch felt pleasure and pride looking at his creations and was excited to share his art with everyone else. The more he tested the Mayhem, the more pleased he became.

Then Lunch was struck by one of those inspirations of genius that sometimes come to the true artist and to those who challenge their own assumptions. He asked himself, *Is it really best that the main player in the plan*—that is, Claudette—*have a clear head?* Heck, after testing another cup of the Mayhem, it became quite clear to him that Claudette desperately needed some loosening up too. And after a few more tastes, he saw clearly how her loosening up would contribute quite nicely to his plan. He pulled out a new bottle of vodka from the mobile liquor cabinet and poured it into the Virginic Delight cooler. He tasted it and found it was not quite what he was looking for. He poured in another bottle of vodka, and after taking another taste, determined this time that it should do the trick.

CHAPTER 15

Unfortunately, as Lunch was testing the un-virginic Virginic Delight again, he didn't notice the three sunglass-wearing, stocking-capped individuals who had just walked up the Strand. They stopped about thirty feet down from the wall that separated the Maison's patio from the bike path.

"Dude," Tree said to Crazy Ahab and Howl, "they're having a party."

"Brilliant, Sherlock," replied Crazy Ahab, "my grandmother could have told us that."

"I wonder what's in those coolers?" said Howl.

"Just hang loose a minute, and let's watch," said Ahab.

Lunch took one more sample of Virginic Delight before grabbing the two empty bottles of vodka and jogging into the house. Inside, he took off his apron, went to the liquor cabinet, and grabbed two more bottles of vodka. Then the phone in the kitchen rang.

Outside on the bike path, Crazy Ahab leaned over the Maison's five-foot-high patio wall, trying to get a better look at the coolers Lunch had filled. Climbing back down, he said to Tree, "See if you can read what those labels say, I'm not long enough."

Tree tried but wasn't quite long enough either.

"Do it again, and we'll hold your feet," said Ahab.

Eventually, Tree managed to stretch out over the wall with Ahab and Howl holding his feet. This time, he could reach the table where the two coolers sat and turned them so he could read the labels. They dragged him back over the wall.

"One says 'Organic Mayhem,'" Tree said. "The other says 'Virginia Delight.'"

"I bet it says *virgin* something or other," said Ahab. "It means there's no booze in it."

Inside the house, with the phone at his ear and holding the two fresh bottles of vodka, Lunch said to Nicole, "I've got it totally under control, Sweet Pea. The patrons are all out on the beach, and Dolphin and the Dawgs are still down at the breakwater."

On the other end of the phone, Nicole said, "We're going to pick out something for Claudette to wear, and I was thinking about getting a little something for myself."

"Whatever you want, babe," Lunch said. "All I've got left to do is to set up the sound system. I'm on my way down to the apartment now to get my boombox."

"Okay, good," said Nicole. "We'll be there around five, after the hairdressers. Oh, and did you make up some nonalcoholic punch?"

"It's all good," said Lunch, "I'm calling it 'Virginic Delight.'"

"Wait a minute, Claudette wants to say something . . . She says don't start without us—wait until we get there."

"Got it, Sweetie, everything's under control. Bye." Lunch hung up the phone, went outside, refilled the mobile liquor cabinet, and ambled out the gate to get his boombox at Nicole's apartment.

Ahab and the Idiots watched Lunch cruise on down the bike path, not exactly walking in a straight line. "Keep watch," Ahab said, after Lunch had gone about fifty yards, "and whistle if anyone comes."

Ahab walked to the gate and sauntered in coolly, straight toward the ice chest. He opened it and looked in. Then he went over to the mobile liquor cabinet. A smile crept over his face. He took one bottle of vodka and went over to the Virginic Delight and poured the whole bottle in. Then, he did the same thing with the other bottle of vodka. After returning the bottles to the cabinet, he filled the pockets of his cargo shorts with three beers from the ice chest and walked out the gate.

"Let's jet out of here," he said. "We got some planning to do."

CHAPTER 16

While Ahab was turning the Un-Virginic Delight to even more Un-Virginic Delight, on the other coast of the country, another kind of mayhem was brewing. Aunt Clemmie had received a call that morning from the assistant of the producer whose movie script she was writing. Aunt Clemmie didn't mind working Saturdays. In fact, she was planning on spending a good part of the day working on a new book. However, she did not like having her plans interrupted. Her contract called for her to be at the production office Monday through Friday, but her weekends were supposed to be her own. And she particularly wasn't used to a twenty-eight-year-old snot-nosed ignoramus telling her, "Jerry's got to have you over here this afternoon. It's urgent."

After a fairly substantial tantrum, she acquiesced. She and Julia arrived at the production office in midtown Manhattan just after 4:00 p.m., three hours later than she was expected.

The assistant, who liked to be called "Iggy," resembled, as Aunt Clemmie had described him, "a gastropod mollusk" (or in the colloquial, a land slug). He was almost as slick and slimy looking as his boss, producer Jerry Donner. When they arrived, Iggy told Julia to stay in the outer office with him. Aunt Clemmie, however, would have none of that. Not only did she like having Julia in meetings, where she was likely to catch a detail that might have been too trivial for her own attention, but it was also in her compassionate nature to not leave a lamb like Julia alone with a sleazy boor like Iggy. Finally, after some attempt at small talk, which Aunt Clemmie abruptly cut short, Iggy ushered the two of them into Jerry's plush office, which was larger than the typical bungalow at Tranquility Beach.

As Aunt Clemmie and Julia entered, Jerry stood behind his desk with his back to them, looking out on the rooftops of Manhattan. "No, no . . . Maybe," he said into one of his phones. "Got to go."

He punched the End button on the phone's base, and then another, "I'm back . . . No, no, no . . . Well, maybe. Got to go."

With his other hand, he picked up another phone, pushed a button, and bringing it to his ear, said, "I'm back." He listened for at least a second, and then, "No, no, tell him to wait." He turned and raised a finger to Aunt Clemmie, signaling presumably a unit of time—which unit not quite clear. He went on, "Listen, Barry, is this your best and final?" Then after a moment, "I need your *final* final."

He pulled the phone from his ear and, slamming it on its base, hung up. He then hit the intercom button on his desk, "Iggy, if Barry calls tell him I just left."

"Why?" Iggy said over the intercom, "Lard-Ass being a hard-ass?"

"It's not a problem," said Donner. "I think we're in great shape."

Donner finally turned his attention to Aunt Clemmie. "Ms. Hardin, I do apologize for keeping you waiting. Can I have Iggy get you and Julia a drink? Latte, green tea, Red Bull?"

"What is so urgent that I have been dragged down here on my day off?" Aunt Clemmie said, already boiling.

"Oh, we are so sorry for the inconvenience, Ms. Hardin," he said, "but, you know, we thought we'd like to get your thoughts on this right away."

"Please, speak to the point."

"Well, there's just a few issues with the way your plot is turning out."

"What's the matter with the plot? You read the book. You knew the plot when you bought it."

"And with the main character."

"What's the matter with Rex Lee? He's a perfect portrait of villainy and a corrupt mind."

"Michael thinks you haven't made him sensitive enough," he said, referring to the star attached to the movie. "He wants something a little more, you know—introspective—so he can show more of his emotional range and psychological depth."

"Rex Lee was a killer, a thief, a blackmailer, an extorter. He cheated at cards and couldn't spell."

"And Michael would like to see if you could work on the dialogue. It's too terse. The vocabulary's too limited. Surely Rex Lee had some native eloquence. Michael's public expects—"

"Rex Lee didn't get through the fourth grade, though he tried three times. On numerous occasions, his victims had to ask him to repeat himself because he mumbled so much that they couldn't understand what he was trying to steal. A Polish milk-truck driver pleaded with him in Polish, thinking that was his native language."

Aunt Clemmie, who hadn't begun the day in the best of moods, was by this time steaming. Julia was afraid to look over at her and didn't need to to know that if this conversation kept up the way it was going, there would be an explosion. Then Jerry made his worst mistake. He sauntered up from behind his big desk to stand right in front of the chairs where Aunt Clemmie and Julia sat and crossed his arms.

"And there's just one other thing. Michael doesn't like the way he's looking with red hair. He wants to change the name from *Red Hair, Red Blood* to *Blond Hair, Bruised Heart*. After all, the environment he grew up in, you know."

That's about as far as Jerry got. In general, Aunt Clemmie wasn't open to criticism about her plots, her characters, or her dialogue, but she absolutely would not tolerate attacks on her titles, many of which had taken weeks to come up with.

Her large leather purse was resting on the floor to her left— you will recall that she was left-handed. In one motion, she rose from her chair, snatched up the purse, and swung it round, smacking Jerry along the right side of his head. He didn't fall over, but he did stagger back into his desk, knocking over his can of Red Bull.

"No one molests my titles. Come, Julia. Mr. Donner can find himself another writer." As they left the room, they abruptly bumped into Iggy, who had been listening at the door.

At the elevator, Aunt Clemmie realized that they would be needing transportation back to California. "Julia, my dear, please go back in there and tell Mr. Iggy that we will need our private coach for the trip back immediately. Remind him that the contract calls for transportation via private car to and from my place of residence."

Julia bravely reentered the office, her boss's behavior emboldening her, or perhaps because she was armed. She also carried a sizable bag, in which she kept a large notepad, numerous writing utensils, and a heavy appointment book. As she opened the door, she saw Jerry Donner, rubbing the side of his head, standing in the outer office with Iggy.

"Ms. Smoote will be requiring the private coach to take us back to California," Julia said, having learned well the imperious style. "Tomorrow morning should be sufficient."

"You can tell that old battle-ax that she's out of her mind if she thinks she's getting a private coach back to California without finishing the script," Donner said, and then walked back into his office and slammed the door.

Julia pulled a copy of the contract out of her handbag and read to Iggy. "It says right here that any and all script modifications must meet the approval of Ms. Smoote." Then turning a few pages over, "Transportation by private railroad car to and from Ms. Smoote's residence in Tranquility Beach, California, to be provided by the Studio."

At this, Iggy laughed. "Why don't you tell your boss you'll be along later, and you and I can go down to happy hour at Freddy's?"

Julia carefully put the contract back in her handbag. Then, in a perfect imitation of Aunt Clemmie, she whacked Iggy along the left side of his head—Julia was right-handed. The blow from her bag, which was considerably heavier than Aunt Clemmie's owing to all the things inside, knocked Iggy off his feet. "If that coach isn't ready for us tomorrow," she said, "I'll start an action against you for unwanted, totally gross advances, you slimy hodad. You make me want to barf!" She slammed the door as she left.

CHAPTER 17

At the Redondo Beach breakwater, the waves peeled off the jetty in perfect lefts. A nasty storm off the coast of Mexico had stirred up a big south swell, generating, when it hit the Southern California coast, consistent eight-foot bombers. It was low tide; the waves were not only "twice overhead" but were steep, hollow, and tubular.

Ordinarily, on days like this, Dolphin would be tearing the place apart. He was the strongest paddler around and would be catching more waves than anyone, taking off close to the jetty, hanging back in the curl, milking the wave past the false section, and carving all the way into the shore break, down past the Chart House Restaurant. And then after a few minutes, he'd be back in the lineup, getting his pick of the next set.

But today he seemed to be someplace else. A big set loomed two hundred feet beyond the setup, and he didn't even notice or care or move, even with everyone paddling like crazy to get past it and yelling, "Outside!" He got crunched and seemed to enjoy it. On the next set, he managed to get in position and caught the wave of the set. But after an extremely radical no-paddle late takeoff that he very nearly got mangled on and cranking a bottom turn that two of his three fins came out of the water on, he hung back, farther and farther into the tube, finally getting swallowed in the "green room," as it is called.

A few minutes later, Dolphin sat on the beach on the tail of his surfboard. Easy Dog had come up next to him to cheer him up but was not successful. Fast Eddie and Easy Ed came out of the water, carrying their surfboards, and walked up to their friend.

"You guys were tearing it up out there," Dolphin said. "Dudes, you ought to stay out."

"Dawg, I saw that last wave of yours," Easy said. "You were so far back in the tunnel I couldn't believe it. It must have been twelve feet. You could have made it out, but you just let the wave suck you back and eat you. It looked awesome. I've never seen anyone swallowed so bad."

"It was one of the most casual calamities I've ever seen," Fast said.

"Yeah, it was fun," said Dolphin, patting Easy Dog, who was trying to console him by licking his legs. "I got caught inside twice too."

"Dude, are you sure you're alright?" asked Fast.

"I just got other things on my mind. You guys ought to go back out. It was awesome watching you."

"Claudette?" Easy asked.

"I just can't stop thinking about her."

Easy gave a knowing look to Fast. "We're supposed to help Lunch get ready for the barbeque. We're going to go back and give him a hand."

"It's cool—I'll go back and help him," said Dolphin. "You guys can stay longer."

"No, dawg," said Easy, "we've got to get back too. We can let those other dudes have a few waves. As security director, I want to make sure nobody tries to crash our party."

CHAPTER 18

Shaded by an umbrella, three of the patrons, Mr. Mallow, Sergeant Snipe, and Ms. Root, sat at a large table on the Maison's patio. Lunch was in the kitchen preparing meat for the barbeque, and the Dawgs had not yet come back from the beach. Mr. Wiley was still up in his room.

"We're getting close," said Ms. Root. "We've done a good job. He doesn't appear to be showing much interest in any of us."

"I can see why he hasn't shown any interest in *you*," said Mr. Mallow.

"I'm trying to tone it down, but I think I have a gift for acting frumpy."

"You're doing fine," said Sergeant Snipe. "Just give me a little more time. Another few nights, and I should have enough traces for what we need. I think Marshall's the one who's putting it on a little too thick."

"He doesn't like former accountants," Mr. Mallow said. "He's hardly said a word to me. Anyway, I need more time. The numbers are very complicated."

Ms. Root said, "Okay, I think we have time. But don't put it on too thick. And please watch your alcohol."

"Well, speaking of that, I think I am going to give that Virginic Delight a try," Sergeant Snipe said. "It looks quite healthy. Can I get y'all a cup while I'm at it?"

A mile and a half up the bike path and down one of the side streets, Crazy Ahab and the Village Idiots were putting the final touches on their plan. Earlier that day, Ahab had instructed Howl to cruise by the Sandcastle and do a reconnaissance mission. "Try to get a look at the renters," he had instructed. "We don't want any of them to be so old that we give 'em a heart attack. And make sure the fuse box is where I remember it, back on the wall by where they park the cars."

Tree had now returned, reporting that he had seen three of the renters, saying, "They look sturdy enough," and, "One of them was kind of buff, though he was wearing short shorts."

"Did you find the fuse box?"

"Yeah, it's right where you said it would be, next to where they park the cars. Only one car was there. A big blue Ford."

"Did you check the license plate? Did it look normal? With what we're doing tonight, it wouldn't do to have any cops around."

"It looked normal enough to me," Howl lied, having not taken the time to check out the car.

Mr. Wiley had now joined the rest of the patrons at the table on the patio, and Lunch had come out to see how they were faring. All four of the patrons were holding sixteen-ounce red plastic party cups and appeared to be enjoying at least some version of Lunch's organic concoctions. An atmosphere of congeniality had indeed settled on the partygoers, with even Mr. Wiley becoming more communicative. A few minutes after four, an hour before Claudette's schedule, Lunch decided to start showing off his music collection.

He, like Claudette, also wanted the patrons to feel comfortable and wanted them to converse freely. As he was responsible for providing music for the party, he had planned a little game based on the patron's music preferences. On his own initiative, he had sent out a note the day before asking the patrons to bring to the party a sampling of the types of music they most enjoyed. A person's music preferences can be quite revealing, providing a window into a person's soul, so to speak. Chatter about their favorite music, along with his punch, Lunch thought, would lead to everyone lowering their inhibitions and would get the party going. He even thought to mix in a few of his own favorites to spice things up. He was quite proud of his music collection and enjoyed showing it off.

Lunch's musical tastes, however, were an arguable subject. His taste *in* music was debatable, but his taste *for* it—or, more properly, his *appetite* for it—was almost as great as his appetite for fun and food. He had a collection of thousands of recordings, of almost every genre.

Lunch would probably want to make one small disclaimer: in his broad appreciation of music, there was a new trend that he had difficulty tolerating. It was called, "emo." He got a strange compulsion, when he came across a devotee of this whiny display of sentiment, to drown him like an unwanted rodent, or at least scare him enough to make him cry, which likely wouldn't take much to do, proving his position.

Of course, it was only in the Walkman era that Lunch's appetite for music could be so fully indulged. Lunch had a collection upward of fifty thousand titles that he had copied onto reel-to-reel tapes. Whether he had obtained these within the strict letter of the law is anyone's guess. But he did have a vast and varied hoard in almost every category imaginable, except, of course, emo. And with the responses he received from the patrons, he prepared a couple of handfuls of cassettes for a game that he would play with the patrons at the party.

After he made sure everyone had a fresh drink, he proceeded with the challenge: "Mr. Mallow, let's start with you, what's your bag when it comes to music?"

"Oh, do please call me Marshall," he replied, pulling a sheet of paper from his shirt pocket. "I hope you don't mind, but I was so interested in your question I jotted down a few notes to make sure I covered the salient points of my feelings on the subject."

"Shoot the moon," said Lunch, and the other patrons didn't seem to mind either, though upon hearing Mr. Mallow's use of the term "salient points," Ms. Root almost spat out a mouthful of what she thought was Virginic Delight. She quickly regained her composure.

Mr. Mallow cleared his throat and read: "In regard to the ineffable subject of music, I have wide and eclectic tastes in the 'language of the gods.' It is foolish to rank one type or artist above another—one shouldn't judge—but as Kant has taught us, categorization is inevitable. For brevity's sake"—at this point he took a big gulp from his cup and, putting it down, spilled some of its contents on his paper—"my tastes incline to earlier times, and thus, I have a definite inclination toward speed metal. Grand Funk Railroad, for instance, and more currently, Iron Maiden. Next, I will always appreciate early punk, so well represented by . . ." Here he paused, trying to read his notes, which was difficult because of the spilled punch. "Oh, yes, the Mothers of Calamity."

"I think maybe you mean the Mothers of Invention," said Lunch. "I think it's a stretch to say that they were early punk. But they did go through some interesting phases."

"Yes, of course, the Mothers of Invention," Mr. Mallow said.

"Can't say I'm familiar with them, but I do like the concept," said Mr. Wiley, who had just returned from filling up Mr. Mallow's cup for him. "Necessity is the mother of invention and a whole lot of other things. I consider myself something of an inventor."

Mr. Mallow took a swig from his newly filled cup, "Well, going on, I have to confess that I was not left unfazed by the disco craze. I still know of a few clubs in Seattle that I frequent whenever I find myself there."

"Seattle?" blurted Ms. Root. "Seattle's known for grunge music."

"Grunge and disco," answered Mr. Mallow. "A fine line between the two. Grunge evolved out of disco. This new band up there—their name is taken from the mental state that the best disco dancers achieve—started in disco. They've evolved a bit, changing their wardrobe with the times. But their musical roots are still evident.

"Lately, my musical interests have turned to international hip-hop. And here is my challenge," Mr. Mallow said, his countenance turning serious, "do you, Mr. Biggunes, have anything from Vladi and Warmints, an underground Czechoslovakian group?"

All eyes turned to Lunch. "Really trying to stump me, Marshall." Lunch said.

"I play to win," Mr. Mallow rejoined.

"Well, okay, if Vladi and Warmints is what you're going to challenge me with, you need to give me a song."

"How about 'Wolga Shuffle'?" said Mr. Mallow.

"That's what you want to go with?" Lunch said, trying to show concern.

"I'll go with it."

Lunch looked through a number of his cassettes and picked out one and placed it in his boombox. He pressed Fast Forward for a few seconds then pressed Play. A male voice yodeling came on. Lunch quickly pushed Fast Forward again, then the Play button. Something that sounded like white-boy rap mixed to a polka rhythm started up, with the words first in Czech, then in English:

> *A moj, moj, moj pritelkyne*
> *Ona nemiluje me pro ze*
> *Ale miluju ona, Ale miluju te*
> *Mozna jeste jednou pivo pro me . . .*

> *And my, my, my girlfriend*
> *She doesn't love me for this*
> *But I love her, But I love you*
> *Maybe one more beer for me . . .*

"I surrender," said Mr. Mallow.

"You have quite a variety of music there," said Ms. Root.

"I have a lot more at home, and just in case any of you are cops," he said, laughing at the idea, "most of it is legal."

Just then, Dolphin, Fast, and Easy walked in through the gate in board shorts with their surfboards.

"Dawgs, you're here," said Lunch. "You were out in the water for a long time!"

"It was totally rad, dude," Easy said. "I've never seen Dolphin get so deep in the tube—course he didn't come out. It just may have been the most casual wipeout I've ever seen."

"Awesome!" said Lunch, taking a drink. "We're just getting better acquainted here. Get yourselves a drink. There's beer, and in the coolers there's something I invented, inspired by my time in the Islands, called Organic Mayhem. The jug on the left is the variety without the nitroglycerin," he said, this time forgetting he had previously spiked the punch.

"Dude, sounds awesome," said Easy. He put down his surfboard and poured himself and the other Dawgs a cup.

"I'll just stick with the virgin stuff," said Dolphin to Easy. The three took their drinks and went off to the courtyard to shower and put their surfboards away.

"This stuff is really refreshing," said Dolphin, after he had stowed his board in the locker under the balcony, "even without the firewater."

"You oughta try the batch *with* it," said Fast.

"This is good enough for me," said Dolphin, who had been bluer than the sky, but now started livening up. "We got to keep our eye on Lunch. He's getting loose. It's a good thing that Claudette isn't going to be here. She'd kill him."

Fast and Easy gave each other a knowing look.

"Good thing," said Fast.

"Yeah, good thing," said Easy.

After the 'Wolga Shuffle' ended, Lunch turned to Ms. Root. "Now it's your turn, Cloris. What's your bag when it comes to tunes?"

"Oh, dear," said Ms. Root, blushing and taking another swig of her drink. "If you really want to know, I'm a Wall of Sound person, most anything that Phil Spector produced in his heyday, before he purportedly shot his girlfriend. And the people who copied him—that is, his music, not in shooting his girlfriend—you know, like the Ronettes, the Dixie Cups, Martha and the Vandellas—'Dancing in the Street,' that type of thing. My older sister was really into *American Bandstand*, and I just got hooked on the stuff. That's where I learned to dance too. Oh, let me see, 'Chapel of Love' is another one I really like, 'Da Doo Ron Ron' too, and another is 'My Boyfriend's Back.' I'm still just waiting for him to return." At this, she laughed.

Mr. Mallow gave her an amused look.

"That stuff is bitchin'," Lunch said.

"Indeed!" Mr. Mallow agreed after taking a gulp from his cup. "But Cloris, give me something harder than that!"

"'Johnny Angel'?"

"Oh, how I love him," sang Lunch, surprising everyone how high his voice went in imitation of the song. "Got it. Shelley was such a babe."

"'It's My Party, and I'll Cry If I Want To'?"

"Easy."

"'Only Love Can Break a Heart, Only Love Can Mend It Again'?"

Having put their boards away and showered, the three Dawgs now walked back into the patio and sat down.

On hearing this last title, Dolphin said, after refilling his cup with what he thought was nonalcoholic punch, "Tee that one up for me. Sounds like my kind of song."

"I'm down with Gene Pitney, but too easy," said Lunch. "Try again."

"The Stone Poneys—'Long, Long Time,'" said Cloris.

"That is a great but very sad, sad song, Cloris."

"Play it, dude," said Dolphin. "The sadder the better."

"That song's too sad to play at a party. I'll play something else from Linda." Lunch launched 'You're No Good' and got up and did a kind of a pharaoh-jive step dance to the beat as he wandered back to the refreshment table.

"I give up," said Ms. Root.

CHAPTER 19

At about the same time in New York, Julia was in the rear of the lobby of her and Aunt Clemmie's hotel at a row of pay phones. She had told Aunt Clemmie she was going down to call her mom and tell her about her first trip to Manhattan. She had first bought some Peanut M&M's from the hotel market and asked for the change from her five-dollar bill in quarters.

"Eddie," she said into the phone after she had dialed and deposited the ten quarters. "Eddie, pick it up. Answer, you dolt! Answer."

She heard Easy Ed's answering machine greeting: "You reached Easy, so take it that way and leave a message."

"Eddie, it's me," Julia said. "Aunt Clemmie just quit her job! We're coming back! We're going to be back five days from tomorrow—five days! Tell Dolphin, you guys have to get those renters out of there or you're all toast! Understand—in five days we're going to be back!"

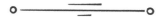

By the time Linda Ronstadt had reached the last chorus of 'You're No Good,' everyone at the party, including Dolphin, had joined in. Not quite, but approaching the top of their lungs, they sang, "Baby, you're no goooooood." They gave each other a round of high fives. Lunch gave out a Hawaiian war whoop of "Ahouutah." Then they sat down again, and all eyes turned to Sergeant Snipe to discover his musical bliss.

"You're up, Sarge. Just what tunes floor your throttle?" said Lunch.

"Well for me, as you may have guessed from the timbre of my voice, there's nothing like the crooners."

"The which?" said Fast Ed.

"Before your time, son. Before mine too," said the sergeant. "An old drill sergeant of mine in basic turned me on to them: Perry Como, Dean Martin, Sinatra. Nothing soothes the nerves after a night patrol in the jungle like the crooners. And of all the crooners, for me, Boone is the man."

"Daniel Boone?" asked Dolphin.

"Not that old—*Pat* Boone, especially early Boone. I hear he got into rap or something later—that's not my cup of sake. But if you've got 'Love Letters in the Sand,' you are absolutely the man. I was sitting out on the beach the other day, watching the waves wash up on the sand, and I could hardly hold back the tears. Reminded me of this little Japanese dish I knew in Okinawa."

"Dude, Boone is totally awesome," said Lunch, giving Snipe a high five. Lunch was stoked he had found another person who liked Pat Boone, and he was now extra glad that they hadn't chosen Snipe to make Dolphin jealous with Claudette. He even forgave him for his unstylish survival stance, which reminded all the Dawgs of Crazy Ahab's surfing style.

"Actually, Boone tried to make a comeback a few years ago, doing some metal stuff," Lunch added. "It was okay, but nothing compared to 'Letters'"

"Dude, I have an autographed picture of that cat," said Easy. "My dad used him in some infomercials once. He's probably sixty by now, but he looks like he's twenty-five." Easy had forgotten that he didn't like people to know that his dad made infomercials—it being a Hollywood type of thing.

"I'd be interested to know what antiaging techniques he uses," said Mr. Mallow.

"When we were in fifth grade, we used to dress like Pat Boone," said Lunch. "Those soft white buckskin shoes were so comfortable. He started a revolution in footwear! Dude, Nike oughta be paying him royalties."

Everyone high-fived everyone else and whooped and hollered even though only about half of them had ever heard of Pat Boone, and no one except Lunch knew anything about his footwear, though everyone agreed Nike ought to be paying him royalties.

Across the way, on the other side of the bike path, the sun dipped into the sea, its fading glory mixing with the smog that poured forth, creating a wondrous pallet of orange, blue, green, purple, and brown across the sky. And in contrast to that beauty, behind the wall enclosing the Maison's patio, Crazy Ahab, Tree, and Howl, stocking caps pulled down to their dark glasses, leered at the party.

"Look at Biggunes," Ahab said. "I think he's having a flashback."

"They're getting bombed," said Howl. "It's not like the Dawgs to get that bombed."

"It's that vodka I poured in their punch," Ahab said.

"Should we do it now?" asked Tree.

"No, dude, still too early," said Ahab. "We got to wait till it gets dark."

"If you have a karaoke machine," Sergeant Snipe said, when the chatter about Pat Boone and Nike's debt to him died down, "I have a number of his classics in my repertoire."

"Don't have one," said Lunch, "but you can croak along with him once I tee him up. Maybe I'll even join you."

Then Dolphin raised his mug. "To the mellifluous voice of Sergeant Snipe." This was followed by another chorus of cheers by everyone.

"Where'd you get that word?" asked Fast Eddie. "You probably don't even know what it means."

"'Course I do," said Dolphin. "'The mellifluous voice of the silent orbs'—I wrote that treacle in seventh grade. It means sweetly flowing. I was in my Miltonic stage then." During Dolphin's seventh and eighth grade years, Aunt Clemmie took his education into her own hands and homeschooled him. Every once in a while, Dolphin would inadvertently let some of those seeds of learning sprout out.

"And you, Mr. W?" asked Lunch, turning his attention to Mr. Wiley. "You don't mind if I call you Mr. W, do you?"

"Not at all, son. We're in California, aren't we?"

"Mr. W, just what gets your ya-yas out?"

"To my tastes," said Mr. Wiley, "sad cowboy and outlaw songs can't be beat. And the ones where somebody dies are the saddest."

"Do they always have to be so sad?" asked Ms. Root.

"Mostly. It does help. 'Streets of Laredo,' 'El Paso,' 'Mama Tried,' and probably my favorite, 'Mother, the Queen of My Heart.' That's 'bout a boy who goes wrong and lets his poor old dying mother down. Gets me right here." Wiley patted himself on the chest and wrestled to hold back his emotion.

"My old man turned me on to Jimmie Rodgers, the Singing Brakeman, when I was a kid," said Lunch. "He used to ride the rails a little himself. Maybe even still does, for that matter."

"My grandpa used to sing a song about this guy's old dog dying," said Easy. "It used to make me cry and have nightmares."

Mr. Wiley cleared his throat. "I wouldn't be lying if I told you lately I've also become a big fan of surf music. I see a lot in common between Southern California and Texas—between cowboys and surfers—that's one of the reasons I like spending my summers sailing the West Coast. Talking about that, I just can't figure out why your USC Trojans picked a name like that for their mascot. Now *Long Horns*—that's a name. But *Trojans*? They lost the dern Trojan War, if you recall. Fell for that stupid trick of the wooden horse and all. Must have been morons—or drunk. I reckon if they called themselves something else, they might do better."

"I appreciate your perspective, Mr. Wiley," said Ms. Root. "I'm a Texan too—a UT grad."

"Well then, hook-em, sister," said Mr. W, giving her the "hook 'em" sign, an outstretched thumb and little finger.

"Hook 'em your own self," she said, returning the sign and demonstrating that the Mayhem could loosen anyone up.

"Mr. W, let me just say, if you like surf music, your momma would be proud of you," Dolphin said.

"Well, son, thank you for saying it. I appreciate it. I only wish it were the case."

"You went to UT?" Dolphin asked Ms. Root. "What did you study there?"

"Forensics," Mr. Mallow blurted.

Ms. Root kicked Mr. Mallow under the table. "A lot of good it's done me." Just then the gate opened and in walked Nicole and Claudette.

CHAPTER 20

It wasn't clear if anyone paid attention to the last few bits of conversation, as all the men's attention shot immediately to the two ladies, especially the tall brunette, who had just walked in the gate. A spontaneous outbreak of "wahoo" or something like it roared from most of the male partiers. As he was used to seeing Claudette dressed as a butler, Dolphin didn't at first recognize the person who had followed Nicole in, and after he did, he wobbled and fell out of his chair.

She was more beautiful than he had ever seen her before. Still holding his cup, Dolphin had difficulty getting up, but Fast Eddie, sitting next to him, casually plucked him up by his collar and set him back in his chair.

Both girls were not pleased with the scene. "I see you've gotten started early," Nicole said, shooting Lunch a look that could have cut diamonds. "I'd like everyone to meet my friend, Claudette. We'll be in the kitchen." They stormed off.

"Did I say what else I liked about Southern California?" Mr. W said.

Dolphin tried to follow them, but Easy grabbed him and yanked him back. "I'm only getting another drink," Dolphin said. His friend let him go. After filling his mug, he darted off toward the house.

"Don't be easy on him," Nicole whispered to Claudette as Dolphin strode into the kitchen, where Claudette and Nicole were readying the food.

"I thought you said you were going to a funeral," Dolphin said.

"My Granny wasn't dead after all. It's just a trick she uses to get sympathy. She does it all the time."

"Maybe I should try it."

"You weren't supposed to start till Nicole and I got here."

"I didn't even know you were coming."

"That's no excuse. You shouldn't have started anyway. You're all getting sauced! I thought the *so* casual Surf Dawgs could hold their liquor!"

"Lunch made two batches—there's no alcohol in this one," he said, lifting his almost full cup.

Claudette grabbed the cup and took a sip. "That's good," she said, and almost drained it. "Now get out of here. And send EE and FE in here to carry the appetizers out. And have them bring me and Nicole a couple cups of this punch. And make sure it's not the kind with the alcohol. Now get."

Dolphin saluted and trudged off. He was used to Aunt Clemmie yelling at him to get out of the kitchen, so he wasn't offended at getting told to scram. But her behavior bewildered him. He decided she needed to loosen up a little, and so could Nicole for that matter. Instead of sending in a couple of cups of Virginic Delight with Easy and Fast, he had them bring two cups of the Mayhem.

CHAPTER 21

The sun had been down for a half hour by the time Claudette and Nicole returned to the patio. Easy and Fast had made several trips to and from the kitchen bringing out trays of appetizers, the chicken and steaks for Lunch to barbeque, salads, and a big sheet cake the girls had bought at the local bakery and decorated themselves with loads of whipped cream, extra frosting, and a big "Welcome Friends" written on it. The party now was about ten times louder and rowdier than they had planned. Lunch was playing "The Jolly Green Giant" on his boombox while dancing at the barbeque, grilling the meat. Five of the Dawg's friends—three girls and two guys—hearing the sounds of the party, had cruised over, and Easy had allowed them to come in. Emily, all dolled up, had also arrived and was glomming on to Dolphin.

Claudette at first didn't notice Dolphin and the girl who was giving him attention. But by the time in the song when the Kingsmen sang "He stands there laughin' with his hands on his hips, and then he hits you with a can of beans," Claudette was irate. Alcohol affects different people in different ways: some it makes more affable, some witty, some morose, some ornery, some more aggressive, and some more mentally focused, as Churchill said champagne affected him. The influence alcohol had on Claudette at that moment was something of a mix of the latter three: she grew exponentially more indignant than she already was, she rapidly started thinking of ways she might inflict pain and annihilation upon her rival, and her mind became absolutely focused on it. Fortunately, Nicole was alert and grabbed Claudette as she started to charge at Emily.

"Be cool! Remember the plan!" she said.

"That's that little hussy who overcharged us for making the flyers," Claudette seethed.

"Calm down," said Nicole. "You're ten times more pretty than she is. We have to stick to the plan."

"Okay, okay, I'm under control," Claudette said. "Where is that big hunk, Mr. Wiley?"

At that same moment, Crazy Ahab, Tree, and Howl, dressed in black, crept along the side of the house toward the circuit breaker. They stopped, and Ahab flashed his penlight at the box on the wall. He lifted the cover and pointed at the master lever.

"In exactly three minutes," he whispered to Tree, making a motion of pulling the lever down. He shone the light on Tree's watch and put three fingers up in front of his face. Then he handed him the light, and he and Howl crept off.

At Ms. Root's request, the stereo was now blaring "He's a Rebel" by the Crystals. Lunch still danced with the barbeque, now with his back to it, but wasn't totally neglecting the chicken and steaks. Clustered around him were Fast, Mr. Mallow, and three of the newcomers as well as Claudette, who fawning over Mr. Wiley. The other group, at the other end of the big table where the cake and all the appetizers sat, was Sergeant Snipe, Ms. Root, Easy, the two other newcomers, and Emily, who was trying to hang on to Dolphin. The music pulsated loudly, and everyone was throbbing in time with the blim-blam of the boombox. Everyone except Dolphin that is, who in spite of wearing Emily like a bling chain, wouldn't take his eyes off Claudette and Mr. Wiley.

"Why, Missy," Mr. Wiley said to Claudette, as she backed off from him enough to take a pull on her not-so-virgin drink, "this is turning into quite a party."

Mr. Wiley didn't catch Claudette's response, maybe because she slurred it, or maybe because her face was pointing toward the sky, going back and forth like a swivel fan. Mr. Wiley didn't mind; he just continued doing his strange, out-of-rhythm version of the Texas Two-Step.

Crazy Ahab and Howl sneaked along just outside the gate leading into the patio. The music now bellowed out "Wooly Bully," another of Lunch's favorites. It was loud, even on the other side of the wall. Crouching down, Ahab pushed the button on his watch that lit the dial and read the time. Out of his jacket pocket he pulled something that looked like a huge cherry bomb. It was, in fact, a Ping-Pong ball painted red that he had filled with the powder of a string of sixty Black Cat firecrackers and stuffed with a four-inch fuse. Crazy Ahab looked at his watch again.

When Dolphin saw Claudette put her arms around Mr. Wiley's neck, he had had enough. He reached around and undid Emily's hands, which were clasped behind his neck, and more or less dropped her on the patio. He had taken a couple of resolute steps toward Wiley and Claudette, when Easy tried to stop him. Easy had as much effect as he would have had trying to hold back a battleship with a pair of tweezers. Dolphin surged on toward them.

Crazy Ahab lit the fuse on his bomb. He counted, "Five, four"—at which point the lights all through the Maison went out; the patio went black, except for a small LED on the boombox. Ahab stood up just enough to see where he was aiming and arced the mini bomb into the patio.

Dolphin was just raising his hands to strangle Mr. Wiley, when Sergeant Snipe, ever alert, yelled, "Incoming," and jumped into his survival stance.

The bomb landed squarely in the middle of the amply frosted cake. It fizzled for a moment, and then exploded in a terrific blast, shooting frosting and cake everywhere and on everybody. It also shot what was left of the guacamole, the seven-bean dip, and the onion dip all over the patio and caused what was left of the cake to shoot up eight feet in the air before it landed back on the other end of the table.

In the aftermath, two mounds of bodies lay on the ground, all entangled in one another. In one, counting up from the bottom, lay Emily, Mr. Mallow, Ms. Root, two of the newcomers, and finally Fast, who managed somehow to land on top of the pile.

At the bottom of the other pile were Mr. Wiley and Claudette, atop them were the three other newcomers and Dolphin.

Everyone was adorned with a pallet of whipped cream, red and blue icing, guacamole, and bean dip.

It was Claudette, freeing herself from the protective embraces of Mr. Wiley and the four bodies that not-so-comfortably blanketed her, who had the good sense to untwine herself and go get a flashlight. For about thirty seconds all that could be heard above the barely audible sounds of "I Fall to Pieces" by Patsy Kline were various groans, a few giggles, the sound of a slap, and Ms. Root saying, "Stop that!"

The beam of the flashlight panned the patio and the piles of people who lay covered with cake and came to shine on Lunch Biggunes. Lunch was the only one who had refrained from hitting the deck on seeing the bomb. And he'd paid for it. He was hit not only by cake and bean dip but also nice helpings of barbeque sauce. But it would take more than an explosion in a cake to darken Lunch Biggunes's outlook. "At least we still got the Mayhem," he said.

CHAPTER 22

The next morning, Claudette, dressed in her butler's uniform, was sitting on Lunch's bed with her head in her hands while Lunch paced the room. Her head still throbbed from the night before, but her headache wasn't what concerned her.

"Come on now, it isn't really *that* bad," Lunch said.

"He must think I'm a total jerk," she said.

"No. He just thinks you're different. That's what he likes about you."

Just then, Easy flew into the room, clutching a piece of paper. "Where's Dolphin?" he said with a sense of urgency.

Lunch shrugged his shoulders. Claudette barely noticed him.

"He's probably still asleep," said Lunch.

A few moments later, Fast led Dolphin into the room. "I found him on the lifeguard tower." Dolphin, too, was hungover and depressed, and shy at seeing Claudette in the room.

"If this meeting is to talk about last night," Dolphin said, "I'm sure it was Crazy Ahab and the Idiots."

"How do you know?" asked Claudette.

"We did something similar to them a couple of months ago," said Fast.

"We got bigger problems than that. I got this message from Julia on my answering machine," Easy said. "I wrote it down so you could hear the exact words."

Dolphin took the paper and read: "Eddie, it's me. Aunt Clemmie just quit her job! We're coming back! We're going to be back five days from tomorrow—five days! Tell Dolphin you guys have to get those renters out of there or you're all toast! Understand—in five days we're going to be back!"

All eyes were fixed on Dolphin. His expression turned from a look of hungover nausea to panic, for a second or two, then somehow found a look of serene calm. When the going gets tough, the truly casual get going.

Everyone waited for him to say something.

"This is not a problem," he said, pausing for a few seconds, "that we can't deal with."

"What do you mean, 'not a problem'?" Claudette said. "If the patrons aren't out of here when your aunt gets back, maybe she won't kill you, but something worse . . . And I don't want that."

"Dolphin, dude, you've got to realize this is not good," said Lunch. "If Aunt Clemmie gets back and they're still here, you might as well— I mean, she'll kick them out and make you give all that's left back and make you pay back all we've spent. You know what that means?"

"A steady job until you're ninety," said Fast.

"No matter what happens, I'll still be your friend!" said Claudette. "And I'll go to work too."

"I suggest you take what's left and join the French Foreign

Legion, like you're always talking about," said Lunch. "You need to get as far away from this place as you possibly can!"

"Would you dudes just chill?" said Easy. "Can't you see he really does have it under control? This is the Dolphin we're used to seeing. This is when he's at his best. It's Dolphin surfin' Lunada Bay at twenty feet—it's all good. Right, Dolphin?"

All eyes turned to Dolphin again. He started pacing the room and said, "Let's be cool and not panic. We do have five days. Or . . . When did she call?"

"Last night sometime."

"Okay, we have four days," Dolphin said. Then after pacing a few more moments, he stopped and blurted out one word: "Lice."

"Awesome," said Fast.

"Yeah," said Easy, not knowing at all what Dolphin was talking about but just jazzed by how casually radical "lice" sounded at that moment.

"Lice?" said Claudette.

Lunch wasn't sure what to think but would have agreed with Easy and Fast that his response had style.

"We're going to make them think the house is infested with lice," said Dolphin.

"Okay, I'm starting to get your drift," said Lunch. "Could you give us a little more?"

"We've got four days, right? Okay, we can't force them out, right? They've got a contract, and with Ms. Root being a lawyer and all, they'd probably sue us. So, we have to get them to leave on their own."

"Okay, we're trackin' so far," said Lunch.

"I was just out on the beach. Have you been out there yet?

The red tide came in last night. And you know what the red tide brings with it?"

"The red lice?" said Lunch, Fast, and Easy simultaneously.

"What are you talking about?" exclaimed Claudette.

"The red tide comes in a couple of times a year around here," Lunch explained. "It's actually a type of algae or amoebas or something that colors the water, and there's this kind of water lice that feeds on the amoebas and almost always comes with it."

"You mean we really *are* going to get invaded by lice?" said Claudette.

"No, no, the red lice don't bother you unless you go in the water," said Dolphin. "But the patrons don't need to know that. You know the story of Moses and the plague of locusts? We're going to make the patrons think we're getting hit with a plague of lice."

CHAPTER 23

Mr. Wiley was the first to notice the dull red color of the ocean later that morning. He called for Bertram and asked, "Did I drink enough last night to be hallucinating, or is there another explanation for why the ocean this morning looks like it has turned pink?"

Bertram replied, "Sir, it would be best to bring the matter up with the proprietor of the facility. I will be most pleased to send him up."

"Nothing to get alarmed about," said Dolphin, after Mr. Wiley had posed the question to him. Dolphin was wearing a long-sleeved shirt buttoned up to the neck, long pants, gloves, and a stocking cap pulled down over his ears. "Happens on occasion. Nothing to worry about. Just red-colored algae is all it is. And their little, happy feeding cousins. Hopefully, we can deal with it." In an act of great theatricality, he burst out violently scratching himself on the back of the neck.

"You're sure that everything will be okay?" asked Mr. Wiley.

"I've lived on this beach for fifteen years, and I've seen the red tide many times. And I can't recall anyone who's died from it." Dolphin here broke into a laugh. "Just kidding. Really, there's not much of an onshore wind today, so we're going to be in okay shape." Dolphin gave his right hip about eight hearty scratches. "You might want to wear long sleeves and pants for the next couple of weeks though. Oh, forget I said that. There really is nothing to worry about."

After Dolphin left, Mr. Wiley had an unbearable urge to scratch himself. The back of his pate got the treatment.

On the way down the stairs, Dolphin met Mr. Mallow coming out of his room. He, too, had noticed the color of the ocean. "Saw that the red tide came in last night," Mr. Mallow said to Dolphin. "I've seen it before, in Florida. Do you know how long it's supposed to last? I was hoping to do a little body-whomping today. You know, bodysurfing."

"Yes, I know the term, but please don't do that," said Dolphin, scratching his side just under his ribcage about five times, then his left calf seven times. "Whatever you do, don't go out in the water. The death tide—I mean the red tide—it's a little different here on the Pacific. We don't have the pollutants that retard the bio-collateral."

"The bio-collateral?" Mr. Mallow looked concerned.

"Don't be alarmed, it really is nothing. You're not over forty, anyway, are you?"

"What happens if I am over forty?"

"Oh, nothing that serious. You look like you have the body and the immune system of a man half your age." Dolphin turned but, before starting down the stairs, said, "I have to go see about a couple of urgent matters. It might be a good idea, while you're outside, though, to wear long sleeves and pants. Have a nice day."

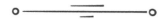

Later that day, Mr. Wiley and Mr. Mallow were sitting at a table on the patio reading in the afternoon sun. They were both dressed like it was winter, with not only full sleeves but also jackets and hats. "There's something they aren't telling us—I'm sure," said Mr. Mallow.

Bertram entered the patio and approached the table. She wore her usual outfit of long pants, coat, and tie but now also white gloves and a Tyrolean mountain hat with earflaps. "Is there anything I can get you, gentlemen?" Bertram asked.

"Quinine," said Mr. Wiley, "That's what they take in the tropics for malaria. Bertram, can you get me a big glass of quinine?"

Bertram suddenly had a very strange expression come upon her face, as if her little finger were being bent back to point at her shoulder. She wrestled with her grimace for a moment and then said, "I beg your pardon, gentlemen, but if you would excuse me for a moment?" She took a few steps away, turned her back to them, and had an outburst of scratching—her thigh first, then her left arm, then the back of her neck. When she had finished, she returned to the table, composed and dignified.

"Quinine, sir, I do believe we have some in the liquor cabinet. Would you like it straight up or on the rocks?"

"Bring us two glasses, no ice, and please hurry," said Mr. Mallow.

When she returned with the drinks, Mr. Wiley didn't beat around the bush. "See here, Bertram, what is going on? What's with this red tide that Mr. Smoote is so concerned about?"

"I am not at liberty to comment, sir. But may I suggest, you speak of the matter with him directly. He is just across the way at the moment." Bertram pointed to the other side of the bike path.

Mr. Wiley's and Mr. Mallow's view of the beach was shielded by a hedge on the other side of the wall, separating the patio from the bike path. Upon rising, they were able to see Dolphin looking out at the ocean with a pair of binoculars. With him were Fast and Easy, also with their backs to the Maison. They all were also intently looking out on the ocean.

Mr. Wiley and Mr. Mallow walked to the wall. From where they stood, they saw Dolphin hand the binoculars to Fast and could hear him say, "It doesn't look good this time. They're thicker than I've ever seen them before."

"The tide is bad enough, why does it always have to bring the red lice," said Fast, scratching the top of his stocking-capped head then behind his ear. "It's the only time I ever wish for pollution. At least it would slow down those varmints."

"It's saying something if you'd rather have pollution than the red lice, isn't it?" said Dolphin. "It's hard for me to judge ages, I just hope none of our patrons are over forty."

"Over forty—heck, if you didn't need me here," said Easy, "I'd just take off for Big Bear for the summer. I'd rather not take any chances."

"But we've developed an immunity, living here all our lives," said Dolphin. "At least we don't get *that* sick anymore. And I always wanted to adopt children rather than have my own, anyway."

"How do you think the lice will affect the patrons?" asked Fast.

"You know what it does to older people," said Easy. "And women at any age."

"I guess I'm obligated to advise them of the risks," said

Dolphin. "And if they want to break their leases, I'll refund a third of their money, including their damage deposit."

"That's honorable of you," said Fast.

"And very generous," said Easy.

On the patio, on the other side of the wall, Mr. Wiley and Mr. Mallow looked at each other. "I think we need to have a talk with Ms. Root and the sergeant," said Mr. Mallow. "I'm afraid this situation is unacceptable."

They found Ms. Root in the living room, trying to pick out a tune on the baby grand piano. She wore a short-sleeved sundress. "Ms. Root," said Mr. Wiley, "do you realize the danger you're in? Here, wrap this around you, and in the future, no bare skin!" He said, handing her an afghan from the sofa.

"I beg your pardon!" said Ms. Root.

Then a loud scream—something between a high-pitched screech and the moaning of a Hawaiian wild pig being prepared to be kaluaed—roared out from the direction of Lunch's downstairs bedroom. The three of them ran off to see what calamity now had befallen.

Bertram was already in the room when Ms. Root, Mr. Wiley, and Mr. Mallow arrived. She was dabbing Lunch's forehead with a wet washcloth, while he shivered violently, though also apparently dripping with perspiration. His whole body, except his face, was under the covers, and approximately where his groin would be, a mound protruded very similar in size and shape to a volleyball.

"He is not doing well," said Bertram, wringing out a quarter pint or so of moisture from the washcloth into a bowl next to the bed. "He doesn't like to admit it, but he's forty-two years old. And this is what happens to those over forty," she said, pointing to the large round protrusion.

"Elephantiasis!" exclaimed Mr. Mallow. "I thought it only happened with mumps."

"I'm okay," Lunch groaned, after a spasm of shivers had passed, "I just shouldn't have slept with my window open."

Dolphin entered the room. "Oh, Roland," said Dolphin, "I should have made you leave when we heard about . . . it."

"Last year, it didn't hit me so bad—I was only down for three months. I knew you needed me, and I couldn't let you down."

"Mr. Smoote," said Mr. Wiley, "may we have a word with you?"

"Let's go into the front room," said Dolphin. The three patrons and Dolphin left the room.

"Mr. Smoote," said Mr. Wiley, "I was not aware of the dangers that accompanied my stay here at the beach, and with the current state of affairs with my business, I just can't afford to miss even one night of work. And, if I can speak for the rest of your guests . . ."

"You can speak for us," said Ms. Root. "We will follow you in your decision, and I hope we can follow you also to a more safe and tranquil summer haven. We so much have enjoyed your company."

"I think," said Mr. Mallow, "that we have no other recourse than to terminate our stay here."

Fortunately, Claudette had been fairly tight with the funds and had so far only spent about a fifth of the three months' advance rent. The patrons were now at the end of their fourth week at the Maison. If Dolphin refunded half instead of a third of the last two month's rent, a decent profit would still be made—close to a thousand dollars for each of the Dawgs—Lunch, Claudette, and Dolphin would get twice that. At a minimum, he could get his car out of the shop.

"As you know," Dolphin said, "the contract which you signed calls for no refund if you choose to break the lease and leave. However, under the circumstances, though I will miss your company, I think it would be reasonable to refund half your rent."

"Of course," said Bertram, who just walked into the room, "that would not include the cleaning deposit."

"That's immensely decent of you," said Mr. Wiley.

At that moment, Sergeant Snipe stormed in through the door, wearing nothing but a tank top and shorts, and carrying an army-green-colored can about the size of a can of whipping cream.

"What on earth are you doing?" said Mr. Wiley to him. "Don't you know the danger you're in?"

"Who's in danger? Not me!" said the sergeant, proudly displaying his can. "I always try to be prepared. You all don't have to worry anymore about the red tide and the red lice. I just so happen to have with my gear a few cans of the 'jungle juice' they used to equip us with in Nicaragua and Panama. They actually developed it in the sixties, before the environmentalists would have had a cow about it. But I do tell you it works. It kills fleas and flies, ticks, mosquitoes, sand lice, crab lice, white lice, rice lice, and any kind of lice I've ever heard of, and about any other living thing you could come across in the jungle or in some nasty little border town. I put it on and went for a dip and haven't been bothered whatsoever. And by the way, I don't think we have to worry about any side effects. Just look at me: I've used it hundreds of times."

"Sergeant, you're a godsend," said Mr. Wiley, "I so much didn't want to have to break up our party here. Please dose me up?"

The good sergeant, proceeded to spray everyone down,

except Bertram, who said he would attend to it himself after he looked in on his patient in the other room.

"I'll be happy to let you use all you need, Mr. Bertram, but if you don't mind, I'd like to do the honor for the good old cook. I've kind of taken a liking to the old boy, and I'd like to spray him down myself." A few minutes later, the sounds of a spraying aerosol can could be heard coming from Lunch's bedroom.

CHAPTER 24

Later that day, in Bertram's room, Dolphin, Bertram, Fast, and Easy met again. Lunch was not present, as he was shopping for that night's dinner.

"It almost worked," Dolphin said. "But we still have three days, plus the rest of today."

"Sergeant Snipe is such a mud hen," said Claudette.

"A what?" said Dolphin.

"It's what my grandmother used to call people who stick their noses into other people's business."

"Was that the grandmother who faked being dead or the daughter of Pretty Boy Floyd?" asked Dolphin.

"Pretty Boy's daughter. I was just kidding about my other granny—the other one isn't faking it."

"Oh, sorry," said Dolphin.

Well, what are we going to do now?" said Fast.

"My cousin in Torrance had the mumps a couple of weeks ago. I could say I got exposed," said Easy.

"Nah. We already used the elephantiasis thing that comes with mumps," said Dolphin.

"How about typhoid fever?" offered Easy. "That's worse."

"That might be a little too drastic," said Claudette.

"And how could we get them to believe that?" said Dolphin, open to nearly any idea but seeing the impracticability of this one.

"If there was only a tsunami coming. Could we fake a tsunami?" asked Fast.

"You've been watching too much news," said Bertram.

"I've got it! Oh, this is going to be sweet. It's perfect," said Dolphin.

"What?" asked Claudette.

Dolphin seemed to enjoy the suspense he was creating.

"Lay it on us, dude," said Fast.

"It's going to be awesome!" Dolphin said.

"Tell us!" said Claudette.

"Ghosts!"

"Did you say *ghosts*?" Claudette said.

"Yes, ghosts!" repeated Dolphin.

"Awesome, totally," Easy said. "I guess we're going to scare 'em out with ghosts."

"That is totally rad," said Fast. "But how are we going to do that?"

"Okay, listen. You know they've been asking a bunch of questions about the house, like why all the corners in the walls are rounded and stuff? And I told them the truth, that the people who built it were afraid of ghosts lurking in ninety-degree corners. And the patrons thought that was interesting, and I'm sure they would like to hear more. Well, after dinner tonight, we'll bring up the subject again, and I'll tell them a story about the house's history. And then, after that, we'll give 'em a night they won't forget."

"You're going to tell them a ghost story about this house?" said Easy.

"Do you know what you're going to say?" said Claudette.

"I'll talk about the dude who used to live here, my favorite surfer in the whole world—SC Parker."

"There's no ghosts in any of the stories about SC Parker that I've ever heard," said Fast.

"Well, there's going to be ghosts in this one, and they aren't going to be nice ones either. Matter of fact, these ghosts are going to be out for revenge."

"This is going to be totally awesome," Easy said, rubbing his hands together.

"It is going to be awesome, but someone's got to tell Lunch," said Fast. "You know how superstitious he is. He's scared of stuff like that."

"I'll tell him," said Claudette. "He should be getting back pretty soon to start dinner."

"Wait a minute," said Dolphin. "We aren't going to tell him. Lunch's not knowing might add credibility to it. If he gets uncomfortable, it might rub off on the patrons."

"That's cruel," said Claudette, "but perfect. He whines all the time about how he wants to go back to his own bedroom. He made me buy him a nightlight."

"Oh, this is just too rad for words," said Easy.

"Okay, no one tells Lunch," said Dolphin. "Now, listen up—this is what we're going to do . . ."

CHAPTER 25

Later that afternoon, the four patrons sat around the table in the dining room, playing a game of whist. As they were engrossed in their game, they barely noticed that on the other side of the door that swung into the kitchen two sets of steps had padded in. Mr. Mallow played a jack of diamonds.

"For heaven's sake, Marshall," said Ms. Root, "it's hearts. If you forget what the trump is again, I'm going to change partners."

"I'm not taking him," said Mr. Wiley. "You've got to play a heart, Marshall!"

On the other side of the kitchen door, another set of feet walked in. Then they heard Bertram's muffled voice saying, "There you two are. I've been looking for you."

Easy's voice answered, "We've been out on the beach."

"Well, we have something of a crisis here," Bertram said from within the kitchen, "and I need your full attention and cooperation."

"Fine," said Fast's voice.

"Do you know what today's date is?" asked Bertram.

"Sure, July fourteenth." This was followed by an exclamation: "Oh, no, the mixture—we were supposed to put the mixture out yesterday!" said Easy.

"Yes, you dunces. Do you have any idea what this means?" said Bertram.

The patrons' game of cards stalled. They all turned and looked at the door that separated them from what was going on in the kitchen and then looked at each other.

"What can we do?" asked Fast on the other side of the door. "We have to do something for, for—well, for *their* sake. We can keep all the windows and doors shut."

"That's not going to help," said Bertram. "Doors and walls don't keep them out. But you're right, we have to try—for their sake. And on top of that, their families would sue us. Come with me, it probably won't work, but we have to try."

"Maybe we should just tell them the truth," said Fast.

"Do you really think they can handle the truth?" said Bertram. Then there was the sound of feet walking and the door on the far side of the kitchen opening and closing.

Back in the dining room, the patrons had put their cards down on the table. "I think there's something else going on here," said Mr. Mallow.

"And they don't want us to know about it," added Ms. Root.

A while later, a number of odd things occurred. Mr. Wiley was back up in his top-floor room and working at his desk with a device that looked something like a small sewing machine, when the door on his balcony suddenly swung open. He got up and shut the door. After a few minutes, he got up to use his bathroom. When he came back, the door was wide open again. He walked over and gave the door a firm closing, making sure it clicked shut. He went back to his desk.

A few minutes later it swung open again. "That's strange," he said to himself, and got up and shut the door again, and this time he locked it.

After a few minutes, a knock sounded at the door of his room. He arose, walked over to the door, and opening it, found Bertram carrying a large plastic bag. "Please pardon the interruption, sir," Bertram said, "but may I visit your balcony for a moment?"

"Not a problem, Bertram, but actually I have been having a little trouble—" Mr. Wiley stopped short because, as he turned around, he saw that the balcony door was wide open again. Then a large black cat came flying—or at least appeared to be flying—into the room, landing on his bed.

Bertram hurried over to the bed and picked up the cat by the hair on the back of its neck and took a few steps toward the balcony. Just in front of the door, while still holding the cat, she put the bag down and reached into it, grabbing a handful of the mixture inside. She proceeded to give the cat a healthy dusting with the mixture. Then she tossed the cat out the door and quickly shut it.

"Trouble, you were saying, sir?" said Bertram, as if what she just did to the cat was as common as turning down the sheets. "You were saying you were having trouble?"

"It's just that door. It won't stay shut. I even locked it and it won't stay shut."

"I am sorry, sir, for the inconvenience. Pardon me for just a few moments."

Bag in hand, Bertram reopened the door and walked out on the balcony, shutting the door quickly, before Mr. Wiley could follow.

Mr. Wiley, pulling the curtain back slightly, looked through the window and saw Bertram sprinkling the mixture all along the perimeter of the balcony with extra doses under the windows and on the doorstep.

"I hope that will suffice," Bertram said, after reentering the room and cinching up the bag she carried. "Please let me know, sir, if you have any more trouble."

"Bertram, wait a minute, what's going on here? What's the matter with my door? And what was with that cat?"

"Cat? Cat? Oh, yes, pesky things, cats. I will mention it to Mr. Smoote."

"What is going on here?"

"Sir, at certain times of the year, we have difficulty with certain orifices of the edifice."

"Jeepers creepers, Bertram, give me a straight answer."

"Sir, I think it would be best to speak to Mr. Smoote about these matters. Please call if I may be of any more service." Bertram hurried out of the room, leaving Mr. Wiley frustrated and confused. He didn't have any more trouble, however, with the cat or his door.

In the kitchen, about an hour later, Lunch began preparations for dinner. His initial idea was for a version of chicken cordon bleu. But at this stage of development, it only barely resembled that. After butterflying ten large chicken breasts, he had stuffed big Ortega peppers with a mixture of chorizo, three cheeses, green onions, and chopped habanero peppers. Finally, he placed those onto one half of each butterflied breast and folded the other halves back over them. He was quite pleased with himself, as he had just invented this dish. He was trying to come up with a name for it when Dolphin walked into the kitchen.

"Mr. Mallow and Ms. Root are out in the living room. Would you mind getting them a drink?" Dolphin asked Lunch.

"I don't know what you figured out to get the renters to leave, but it won't be the food, unless they can't handle habaneros," Lunch said, proud of his creation.

"You're cooking Mexican tonight?" Dolphin asked. "Listen, would you do us all a favor, and for the rest of the month, no more Mexican?"

"It's not really Mexican. It's kind of my own invention—chicken stuffed with peppers, chorizo, and a bunch of cheese."

"I'll tell you why later," said Dolphin, putting an arm around Lunch, "but you'll sleep a lot better if, after tonight, you just don't cook with chilis for a while."

"Why?"

"I'll tell you later. Now, please make Mr. Mallow and Ms. Root a margarita, lots of salt," Dolphin said. He left out the back door of the kitchen.

After Lunch had blended the drinks, he took them out to the patrons, who were in the living room, playing cribbage. After exchanging a few pleasantries, he returned to the kitchen. About two seconds after he returned, a very loud "Who pinched my chilis?" was heard booming out of the kitchen.

Mr. Mallow and Ms. Root converged on the kitchen from one door, and Dolphin and Bertram through the other.

They found Lunch staring at the pan of what was formerly his Ortega-chili-stuffed chicken, but now without the Ortega chilis. Only the butterflied chicken breasts remained in the pan.

"Who took 'em?" demanded Lunch. "Somebody ripped off all ten of my chilis."

"It must have been that," said Bertram, pointing to a big black cat outside the window.

"I thought that window didn't open," said Lunch.

"We just tell people that," said Dolphin. "It's old."

"Since when do cats eat chilis?" said Ms. Root.

"It's a Southern California cat, and our Spanish heritage," said Dolphin. "Cats like chorizo and cheese."

"And what happened to the rest of the tequila?" Lunch blurted out, seeing on the counter that the bottle he had left out after making the margaritas had been drained.

"Oh, now we understand," said Mr. Mallow. "The tequila is missing too. It couldn't have been, Mr. Biggunes, that you just finished it off and have gotten a little confused? That a California thing too? Come, Cloris, let's get back to our cribbage."

"It's okay, Lunch. We'll just order Chinese tonight," Dolphin said.

In about seven seconds, there was another loud cry, this from the living room. Dolphin and Bertram rushed into the room. Ms. Root and Mr. Mallow were holding up their empty margarita glasses. "Three minutes ago, these were full," said Mr. Root, "and we had barely tasted them."

CHAPTER 26

That night, the storm from off the coast of Mexico that was bringing such excellent waves, reached Tranquility Beach. The wind gusted through the palm trees on the Strand, causing them to howl and moan, and the ocean to whitecap far out to sea. Dark clouds hung low and rolled above the boisterous ocean. Rain splattered on the large front windows of the Maison. Thunder cracked, and bolts of lightning skewered the angry clouds. Dolphin couldn't have conjured up a better night to tell his tale.

At dinner, Dolphin told the patrons that due to all their questions about the house and its peculiarities, he would indulge them and share everything he knew about it and its history. With everything that was going on lately, everyone was most interested. After dinner, all retired to the living room, where the patrons took seats on the sofa and Dolphin sat in the big armchair across from them. Bertram took the opportunity to serve after-dinner cordials. Fast and Easy joined as well, and after lighting a fire in the fireplace, took seats on the perimeter of the room. Lunch came in and plopped down on the sofa with the patrons. He had just returned from casing the house to make sure all the windows and doors were bolted.

"As I think you are aware," Dolphin began, "this house isn't exactly your ordinary house, and has what some might find an interesting history. But if you really want to know the full story, and maybe the reason for its peculiarities, you have to know about the land it's built upon."

The patrons mumbled their approval, and Mr. Mallow asked Bertram for a refill of his drink, adding, "I'd appreciate it if you don't let me see the bottom of my glass. The nerves have been acting up a little lately, if you know what I mean."

"Very well, sir."

With that, Dolphin continued. "What I'm going to tell you spans a long period of time, from the misty past of over four hundred years ago up to fairly modern times. Some of what I'm going to say might be mere legend. There's no way to actually prove or disprove that any or all of these events actually did happen. There are probably scientific explanations for everything—even for some of the odd things we occasionally experience around here. Although I don't know if there is an adequate scientific explanation for Lunch Biggunes."

Lunch was the only one who didn't seem to like the joke. He groaned a little and caused his eyes to converge toward the bridge of his nose "That's comforting," he quipped.

"That said," Dolphin went on, "take this tale—especially the older history—with a few grains of salt."

"I saw Bertram sprinkling salt in the corners of walls earlier today," said Mr. Mallow. "Is that what you mean by 'grains of salt'?"

"Actually, sir," said Bertram, "it was a mixture of garlic and salt."

"Oh, it's just kind of a ritual we try to do this time of the year," said Dolphin. "The people who had the house before us also did it, and we figure it's a good idea to follow their example. The only time we didn't do it—well, that's getting ahead of the story. I'll tell you about what happened to poor old Shep when we get there."

"Are you telling me that old Shep's dying was because—" Lunch started to ask before Dolphin cut him off. Lunch was not only concerned because of the affection he had had for the old dog but because he could tell he wasn't going to like this story. He already had too many concerns about the house, and after what had happened earlier in the day, he knew he was going to have a hard time falling asleep that night.

"What really got me interested in the house's history," Dolphin went on, "is when I found out my hero—the greatest surfer, in my opinion, of all time—lived here before my family bought it. His name is, or was, SC Parker. I say 'is or was' because it's not clear if he's still alive—but every once in a while, we do hear rumors of an SC sighting. He was my hero before I found out he lived here, and I set out to learn everything I could about what happened to him, which is how I found out what I am about to tell you.

"SC disappeared sometime around the summer of 1969. He had left California three years earlier, in late July, the reason not fully clear. Some say it was because of the mass of nonlocals who were flooding into the Beach Cities, crowding up his favorite surf spots. Some have even bad-mouthed him, saying that he wanted to put up barbed-wire fences and machinegun nests on all the entrances from the Valley to the beaches to keep the kooks and hodads out."

"Sounds like a reasonable idea to me," said Lunch.

"But that's a lie," said Dolphin. "It was Mickey Gira who said it. SC didn't need to resort to such measures. Even on the most crowded day at Haggerty's or Malibu, he could get all the waves he wanted to himself just by the sheer force of his personality and stature, as well as his tremendous paddling ability. But who would want to take off on the same wave as SC Parker and miss watching liquid poetry on a surfboard? It would be like missing the chance to hear Bach dallying on his clavicle."

Easy and Fast looked at each other. Every once in a while, Dolphin would let loose with something showy like this.

"I think you mean *clavichord*," said Ms. Root. "*Clavicle* is another word for one's collarbone."

"Yes, of course, I did, but anyway, the real reason he left and became a nomad and a wanderer upon the earth was because of Cupid's shaft. Yes, SC left California because of the most painful of all maladies, and the one thing that his greatness of personality and athleticism had no remedy for—a broken heart." As Dolphin said this, he looked at Claudette. He also noticed that talking about a broken heart made his *own* heart feel better. He could understand why there were so many old country songs about broken hearts—singing or talking about it helped the pain to go away.

On hearing about poor SC's broken heart, Ms. Root groaned.

"We know he spent some time in the Midwest," Dolphin went on. "There is evidence of him riding tornado surf in Nebraska, Kansas, and the Dakotas. He won, hands down, the Black Hills Tornado Open two years running, in the falls of sixty-six and sixty-seven. After that, he disappeared again for almost two years, and then there's concrete evidence he resurfaced in Tennessee. He was photographed there riding massive waves generated by dynamited dams that were being demolished from the old Tennessee Valley Authority. I hate to say it, but a lot of the so-called Greenies who are calling for all the rivers to be undammed are just Midwest and Southern surfers looking for big waves." Dolphin paused and took a long pull on his drink, "Well, after that, he disappeared. So, I set out to find out as much as I could about what happened to him."

CHAPTER 27

"My research took me we way back now through the murky tunnels of time, to the history of the piece of land this house is built on, way back to the early 1600s.

"In those days, a freshwater stream flowed close by here from the Dominguez Hills to the ocean. And that is why one of the earliest Spanish padres, Father Pico Pedro Rivera, built his small mission on this very spot. Father Rivera was an awesome old cat who had come north with two other padres early in the century. The two others had died shortly after building the mission, but Father Pico was of a healthy constitution and lived on for over twenty years.

"Anyway, Padre Pico lived a quiet, peaceful, and productive life with the locals on this very piece of land until one sorrowful day. Then—as far I could ascertain—it was in this very month, the month of July, on July thirteenth, 1627, that a set of sails was seen lurking on the horizon."

Isn't that the date today?" asked Easy Ed.

"Yesterday was the thirteenth of July," Bertram said, today is the fourteenth."

"Oh my gosh! we are a day late putting out the—" said Fast Eddy, before Dolphin raised his hand slightly and shook his head an inch or two in a gesture to cut him off. This did not go unnoticed by the patrons.

"It's nothing to worry about," said Dolphin, trying to pass over the subject quickly. "Now, where was I? Oh, yes, the ship was captained by some dude named Capitán Diego Sanchez, who was a drunk. But the big noise of the expedition was the emissary of the Spanish governor, and a real chump. This was the cat who messed everything up for Padre Pico and the locals. His name was Don Arellio de Marcas de Maw.

"Well, when the newcomers landed, this cat, Don Arellio, wasn't too hot with how things were spinning at the mission. Everything was way too mellow for that hotheaded Spaniard. He thought Padre Pico was way too easy on the locals and thought their production from the fields around the mission was way under par. Arellio especially didn't dig that the soldiers who were still alive, who had come up with Padre Pico, rather than going out and finding the Lost City of Gold and the Fountain of Youth, instead were helping out at the mission, getting tan, and trucking with their wives and bambinos, because they had married up with some of the locals and made lots of babies.

"On the other hand, what Arellio did dig was one of the said locals—unfortunately, the wife one of Padre Pico's most loyal followers, whose name, being translated, was Thunder and Lightning, and who when he got riled was more than a little hotheaded himself, as his name implies.

"Well, things didn't start well when the new Spaniards

arrived, and they grew worse. Don Arellio decided that Padre Pico wasn't his main man, so he bound him in irons and chains and cast him into a dungeon he had constructed in the mission's cellar until he could send him back to Mexico to be tortured and burned at the stake."

Here, Mr. Mallow interjected. "Are you saying that the animosity here toward nonlocals goes this far back?"

"Please, Mr. Mallow and my other guests, this is by no means a reflection on you. And besides, as you will hear, there are other issues of concern here. But as I was saying, young Mr. Thunder and Lightning was Padre Pico's most loyal follower, and he wasn't about to let this happen to Padre Pico, who had done so much for him. For you see, before the old padre started his ministrations to Thunder, Thunder was something of a wild child. Thunder had run with the wrong sort and used to steal oranges and avocados from the orchards and sometimes even went swimming in the buff and talked back to his parents and ditched Sunday school if the surf was good.

"Thunder wasn't about to let Padre Pico's chains go unchallenged. He got together a small group of other locals and put together a plan. They realized it wasn't a good idea to try to take Padre Pico by force, because though they could have whipped them in a fair fight, the conquistadores had blunderbusses.

"Now, Thunder had his spies, and you can imagine his concern when he found out that the padre was not really being held in the dungeon but was actually in the hold of the Spanish galleon that Don Arellio had arrived on. So now, with this new information, Thunder had to resort to a radical plan.

"He and his friends talked it over, and they decided they would paddle their canoes out to where the Spanish galleon was anchored and kill the guards and free the padre. Then they would paddle all night with the padre and go hang out with their cousins on Catalina Island.

"Now, the only trouble was that Thunder's wife, whose name was Golden Leaf, who was tall with long golden-brown hair, with gorgeous big brown eyes." Here Dolphin stole a quick look at Claudette to see if she recognized the allusion, her real last name being Leaf and all. And she did, and it was a good thing that the patrons didn't see the look she gave back to him, because they would have thought that there was something strange going on between the butler and Dolphin. "Anyway, Golden Leaf overheard Thunder's plan and thought it would bring sure death to her man and also to her brother, who was part of Thunder's posse. So she tried to get Thunder not to go through with it, but after hours of negotiations, even with all sorts of tears, she couldn't, because Thunder took to freeing the padre as an act of duty and honor. The fact of the matter is that sometimes love and honor clash, and when they do, honor often trumps love."

"You're right, it's true," said Ms. Root. "When a man's honor, is at stake, he will sacrifice anything, even his love, for it. I know the truth of this myself."

"Honor," uttered Mr. Wiley, barely audibly. "What is honor?"

CHAPTER 28

"The next night, Thunder and his boys rowed their canoes out to the ship, all dressed up as Indians, like at the Boston Tea Party."

"But they were Native Americans," Mr. Mallow offered.

"Yes, that's why they were dressed that way," Dolphin said.

"I guess that makes sense, in a way," Mr. Mallow said, still trying to think it through.

Dolphin continued, not wanting to linger on the question. "There were three canoes full of Thunder and his friends, two locals in each canoe. Late at night, they pulled silently up to the side of the galleon, to where the anchor was set. One by one, the six of them climbed up the anchor chain onto the deck of the boat. Each one ducked down and hid by the taffrail until all the rest got aboard. Tomahawks in hand, they snuck along the deck to the door that led down to the hold. Fortunately, a sliver of a moon lit the deck with enough light to keep them from bumping into each other, and also shone down the stairs leading to the ship's dungeon. When five of the six of them had cleared the door, the sixth one of the gang—his name was Lizard—jumped back out and slammed the door shut and bolted it. Lanterns lit up on the deck, and thirty conquistadores carrying blunderbusses came out from hiding. You see, Lizard was a turncoat and had been in cahoots with Don Arellio from the get-go.

"The Spaniards brought Thunder and his friends back to the mission and threw them into the dungeon. It turned out that Padre Pico was down there all along, having been moved to a different cell. Lizard was the one who had told Don Arellio all about their plans.

"Don Arellio set the next day, July thirteenth, exactly one year from when the ship had first arrived, for the hanging of Thunder and his friends. He wouldn't hang Padre Pico, because he wanted to send him back to Mexico to be tortured and burned. Golden Leaf didn't hear about the hanging until she went out in the morning and found her true love's neck stretched on the gibbet with his four friends. She attacked Don Arellio with a knife, and although she might have done some real damage, all she managed to do was cut off the tip of his nose, which peeved him because he was vain and looked at himself in the mirror a lot, and he was planning on putting the moves on Golden Leaf now that Thunder was out of the picture. But as sometimes happens with rejected lovers, Don Arellio's love turned to hate because she made his nose look like a pig's snout. He ended up casting her into the dungeon cell they had been pretending to hold Padre Pico in earlier.

"Well, she was still pretty much out of her mind with grief and couldn't live without her true love and she would have nothing to do with Don Arellio. She managed to poke an eye out of one of the guards, but then he ran her through with a scimitar. Don Arellio, however, claimed she killed herself and wouldn't give her or Thunder a decent burial. He put their heads on pikes on the little bridge that went over the creek, just like they did on London Bridge in the days of Henry the Eighth.

"As I said, that day was July thirteenth, and on the very next morning Don Arellio was found in his bed, dead as a senator's conscience, with a look of fright on his face that would have given Dracula bad dreams. And that look of terror on his face, along with some of the other funny business that happened the same night, caused everyone to think that Thunder and Golden Leaf came back from the dead wandering the earth in chains to even up the score with Don Arellio. The next year on the very same night, the mission burned to the ground, burning alive the new vice-governor and his wife.

"They didn't bother to rebuild the mission either, because everyone was assured it was ghosts that did it and had also killed Don Arellio. They moved the mission inland about thirty miles, and named it Mission Pico Rivera, after the good old padre, and the area around the new mission eventually got named Pico Rivera, and it's still called that today. Padre Pico died a natural death two weeks after everyone was hanged and got buried in the mission yard as Don Arellio wasn't there to deny him a decent burial. But for Thunder and Golden Leaf, it wasn't the case.

"When I finally discovered this, it suggested possible answers to the strange things that happen in this house. It also started to suggest some things about the mystery that surrounded the disappearance SC, the former inhabitant of this house."

CHAPTER 29

On the other coast, a few hours earlier, Aunt Clemmie and Julia, sat in the lobby of their old, elegant, and very expensive Manhattan hotel. On the floor next to them was their horde of luggage. Expecting to leave that morning for Southern California, Aunt Clemmie had finally heard back from Jerry Donner's assistant. And she was not pleased.

Mr. Donner had rescinded his earlier refusal to provide her with a private train car back to Los Angeles. He was rather firm, however, that it would be impossible to arrange for the car until the end of summer, the time clearly stated in their contract. Aunt Clemmie knew that he had her on this one, and she was so mad that she didn't realize how hard she was squeezing the back of her Maltese's neck as it sat on her lap.

The clientele of old, elegant, and expensive hotels tends to be rich, if not always old and elegant. As Aunt Clemmie sat in the lobby stewing over how angry she was, an older, suavely attired, and apparently rich gentleman walked past. After a few steps, he stopped, turned, and stared at her for a moment. Aunt

Clemmie didn't notice, for her mind was deeply occupied with ways she could cause Mr. Donner discomfort.

"Excuse me, mum" he said, using the form of address applied when speaking to the queen of England, "but you wouldn't happen to be Clementine Hardin, the great writer, would you?"

Perhaps she was distracted by imagining how Jerry Donner would react to the Comanche form of torture, because she merely answered yes.

"I beg your pardon, Ms. Hardin, but I am a great fan of yours, and I just couldn't pass by without telling you how much I appreciate your work. My late wife, Elmira, was also a fan. It brought her, and continues to bring me, great pleasure."

"I am honored, I am sure," she said, still distracted.

Looking at the piles of luggage, he said in a friendly tone, "Are you just arriving or departing?"

Aunt Clemmie was still too angry to talk, so after a pause of silence, Julia felt obligated to reply. "Neither coming nor going, sir. There has been a problem with our transportation accommodations back to California."

"Is there any way I may be of assistance? May I have my driver take you to the airport, perhaps?"

"There is a problem with our private coach," Julia said.

Aunt Clemmie tossed her hand out, trying to suggest it was nothing, but rather than suggesting this, it confirmed to the gentleman that she was quite put out.

"I wish I could be of service," he said. "My business will detain me until tomorrow evening, but if you could wait until then, it would be a pleasure to fly you back in my jet."

Aunt Clemmie looked at Julia, indicating her approval. But Julia pretended not to notice. In order to give the Dawgs more time to clear out the renters, she had not been trying very hard to address Aunt Clemmie's "transportation accommodations," as she verbosely called them.

"Ms. Clementine is not comfortable flying," answered Julia. The actual truth behind Aunt Clemmie's distaste for air travel was that she refused to put Louis in a dog carrier. And Aunt Clemmie was not about to charter a plane out of her own funds.

Aunt Clemmie cleared her throat.

Julia smiled.

Aunt Clemmie's throat-clearing turned into a cough.

Julia smiled more and looked placidly about the lobby.

"Are you sure there is nothing I can do for you?" said the older gentleman. "It would give me great pleasure."

"Sir, it is Louis," Aunt Clemmie blurted out, holding up the Maltese, having loosened her grip on the dog's neck. "The reason I don't fly is that I can't bear to see him caged like a common criminal, relatively innocent as he is. I wouldn't think of putting you out, but if you happen to be going close to Los Angeles, and you would not require Louis to be caged, I would be most appreciative of a lift."

"Absolutely," he said. "I am on my way back to Seattle, and if waiting until tomorrow evening suits you, I'd be delighted to drop you off. It's hardly out of our way at all. I'll have my pilot alter the flight plans."

"This is so very kind of you. Tomorrow night would be wonderful."

"But your luggage—have you checked out of your rooms?"

"No, no, that is not a problem. The project I am— well, *was*—working on has reserved them until the end of summer."

"Well then, we'll have you back in California by midnight tomorrow."

"Oh, you are a godsend, Mr. . . . ?"

"Allen—Phillip Allen. But do please call me Phillip."

"And please call me Clementine."

"Oh, I must tell you," said Phillip Allen, turning somewhat grave, "there is one condition."

Aunt Clemmie stiffened. "A condition?"

"Yes. You must be patient with me, for I intend to ask you many questions about your books. Especially about the last one I read, *Slaughter at Midnight*."

"It's a deal, Mr. Allen," said Aunt Clemmie, hardly concealing her pleasure. "You have yourself a deal."

At this, Julia sank into her chair.

CHAPTER 30

Bertram having refreshed the patrons' drinks, Dolphin continued his tale. "After the old mission burned down, nothing else was built on this property until 1912, when some rich dude who made guns bought the property and built a mansion here. He and his wife and young daughter moved in the following summer. Shortly after, one morning in mid-July, while he was away on business, his wife was found dead on the floor of her room. The cops ruled it a heart attack, but her face looked like her life was literally sucked right out of her nostrils, her eyes bulging almost out of their sockets, and her arms frozen as if trying to claw at the air. Her teenage daughter testified she had heard screeching the night before but thought it was a cat fight in the alley.

"The next July, the father died in very similar circumstances. As you might imagine, the daughter, who had been with relatives in San Jose for the summer, took the strange deaths of her parents pretty hard. She had the house demolished. And with all the millions of dollars that she was heiress to, she had this current house built. And that's why the house looks like a big castle—because it was modeled after a castle in Bohemia that was supposed to have the ability to ward off ghosts. That's why there's all these strange features about the house—because they supposedly make the house ghost proof. As you've noticed, there's not a ninety-degree angle in all the house, because in corners of walls, ghosts supposedly can hide. The outer doors are all made of Brazilian Rosewood, one of the hardest woods there is, because the grain causes deep echoes—that's also why it's the best wood in the world for guitars—and when ghosts try to walk through it, the echoing wood gets them all confused. The outer edge of the roof, maybe you've noticed, has spikes sticking upward, taken from some castle in Italy, so the ghosts can't pace about on the edge of the roof, like old Hamlet's pa on the parapet of Elsinore Castle. And she initiated the procedures to start from July thirteenth through the end of the month, making sure to have plenty of the well-known ghost-thwarter scattered around all the outside doors and windows, and in all the corners of the walls—you know, just to be safe.

"Well, anyway, the heiress built this house in this special way, because she blamed it for what happened to her parents. And it seemed that things went reasonably well for the rest of her life, though she never visited the place during the whole of July.

"She died in 1929, leaving it to a man named Rook, who had lived in it as the caretaker since the house was built. And if you think the daughter was a couple cards short of a full deck, this cat had been left out of the deal."

"Did he stay in the house, even in Julys?" asked Lunch.

"Yeah, he's the one that spelled out all the procedures, which he apparently carried out closely, in a long letter he left for the people he sold the house to. Incidentally, that's also where a lot of this history comes from."

"But yesterday was the thirteenth, and you didn't get the mixture put out until today?" asked Lunch.

"Is it really true?" asked Ms. Root. "You didn't get the mixture out until today?"

"I saw them dusting the place this morning," said Mr. Wiley.

"I must take the responsibility," said Bertram.

"Do you really think one day's going to matter?" Dolphin asked. "I've lived here for many years. We've been late before and nothing much has happened."

"How many times have you been late?" asked Mr. Mallow.

"Once, but I was traveling with my aunt."

"So, *that's* what happened to old Shep?" Lunch asked.

Dolphin hesitated.

"Please tell us what happened to your dog," Ms. Root said.

"Well, it was a while ago, when I was in junior high. All I remember is that my aunt was in a hurry to take me to Disneyland for a few days. When we came back three days later, everything was okay except that old Shep, our dog, was dead. And they wouldn't let me see him."

"I was around back then," said Lunch. "That dog was my pal."

"What happened to the man who sold the house?" asked Mr. Mallow.

"Yeah, I was getting to that. Old Rook sold the house to a husband and wife who had adopted this Texas orphan who would grow up to be the greatest surfer the world has ever known: SC Parker.

"Truth be told, SC wasn't a born local, he was an earned local. He was born in Texas. And, as I said, was adopted. His real parents owned a big cattle ranch in the western part of the state and had their own private plane to fly around to see their land. Both got killed when that plane went down in a tornado. And because SC was too young, everything got put into the hands of some distant relatives on his mother's side who sold the ranch and with the money came out here and bought this place 'cause they wanted to get into the movie business, like most of the immigrants. And in order to get control of all the money, they had to adopt SC as their own.

"He was something of a prodigy growing up on the ranch, following in his father's footsteps, and was a top hand for riding and breaking wild horses by the time he was ten. This coming from his Comanche side—he was one-quarter Comanche— and as everyone knows, Comanches were the best horse people on the plains, and probably the best horse people ever. And it just may be that his early experience with riding wild horses is what gave him such great insight and ability in riding waves.

"There's a story about him and what happened just a few months before his parents went down that's worth hearing. It was late spring, and his father and the ranch hands were break- ing some wild mustangs. When SC got home from school that afternoon, there was one stallion left out of the roundup that nobody could stay on. SC was eleven at the time.

"SC immediately ran up and asked his pa if he could give it a try. His dad told him no, at first, but then all the hands said he ought to let him try because he had a way with horses, and some just thought getting bucked off on his head would be good for him.

"So, SC, with some of the hands, put a burlap bag over the horse's head—the stallion's name was Molly—and SC mounted up. Molly took off and flew about six feet in the air, doing a series of one-eighties—one way, then back the other—until it must have gotten dizzy. Then it drew up, and with one last huge buck, sprung eight feet in the air, and all the time, SC was just as comfortable and casual and happy as if he were eating a banana split.

"When Molly came down, she was so tired that she just gave up and was the easiest-riding horse in the whole remuda after that."

"I thought you said it was a stallion?" said Ms. Root.

"I did. And Molly was, and that was why he used to be so mean—'cause everyone called him a girl's name.

"Anyway, not six months after this, SC found himself an orphan living in a strange house with a couple of strange distant relatives who were weird enough on their own but got even weirder as the house started to rub off on them. You see, they were originally from Boston.

"SC was a quick learner and figured out that it wasn't too difficult to live and thrive in his new house and in Tranquility Beach. He quickly learned to surf, helping in those early years to shape the sport. But unfortunately, as SC advanced more and more, becoming the undisputed greatest surfer, the more careless he became, at least at home.

"One summer—by then he was twenty-three years old—he'd been on a surf safari in Denmark, finding unknown surf spots and establishing a huge following in that country. He discovered Rylow Bay, just outside a little fishing village called Johbnhed, a hundred or so kilometers south of Copenhagen. And it was there, in old Johbnhed that SC met the love of his life.

"Her name was Karenina. The day they met, he was out in

the water at Rylow and she was down on the beach standing apart from the admiring crowd. SC was doing a backside cutback on a big almost frozen left, when she smiled at him, and he at her, and as the saying goes, time stood still. Unfortunately, the wave he was on did not stand still, and he slammed into a boat full of paparazzi who were trying to take pictures of him, almost killing him.

"Karenina, with the help of her brother Lars, brought SC home, and when SC awoke three days later, he thought he was still dreaming. There she was, the love of his life, nursing him back to health.

"Well, her parents weren't a problem, because they had heard of SC—as the whole country had—and they agreed to let Karenina go back with SC to visit California and check out Tranquility Beach, as long as brother Lars would go with them to chaperone.

"They arrived back in Tranquility late on the night of July twelfth. SC's adoptive parents were out of town, as they made a habit of staying clear of the house in the summer. They were so cheap they didn't have a caretaker, so there was no one to make sure all the proper procedures were being followed. I guess SC was so much in love he couldn't think straight. Or maybe it was jet lag, and he got his days mixed up. But most of all it was his tragic flaw: hummus."

"I think you might mean *hubris*," offered Ms. Root. "Hummus is a dip made of mashed chickpeas."

"Did I say *hummus*? Slip of the tongue. Meant *hubris*, the flaw of many of the great ones. The point is, it got to be the night of July thirteenth, and they retired early to their separate bedrooms—Karenina to the room that Mr. Wiley stays in now, and Lars to Ms. Root's.

"SC, still recovering from jet lag, couldn't sleep and figured that maybe a good stiff drink would help. So he went downstairs and looked for his favorite drink, which was tequila, but the only thing he found was a bottle of mescal. He grabbed the bottle and a glass and went back up to his room. And from what most of the experts say, that is what saved him. For it turns out that old Thunder had a weakness for tequila, but he wouldn't come close to mescal. No one knows why. Maybe it has something to do with the worm in the bottle. Who knows, but the next morning, both Karenina and Lars were gone, but SC was spared."

"You mean gone as in . . . ?" asked Ms. Root.

"I mean as in *gone*—stone cold, block dead, looking like they got spiked with enough electricity to light up Las Vegas.

"Of course, SC blamed himself—his prideful, foolish carelessness. He was so deeply in love it was like his heart was split in two, Karenina carrying off the other half. Some lesser souls in so much pain might have taken the easy way out and ended it themselves. But not SC—he would stay alive just so his agony would remind him of his love. And he would do great exploits to honor her name."

Breaking the long silence that had followed the ending of Dolphin's tale, Bertram asked, "May I offer anyone a last beverage or snack before I close up the kitchen?"

"Got a little work to do before I can get my beauty sleep," said Mr. Wiley. "Hope whatever bothered old SC and his friends isn't around or at least doesn't give out any frequency interference. Y'all, sleep tight."

"Think I'll adjourn for the evening myself," said Ms. Root.

"As will I," Mr. Mallow said.

"I'll call it a night too," said the sergeant. "Want to be fresh for my morning ten-miler. Good night."

"I hope you have an enjoyable rest," said Dolphin.

As the patrons were departing upstairs, Lunch Biggunes walked off to his room. Arriving, he called Nicole, and she agreed that he could stay at her apartment that night.

CHAPTER 31

Later that night, Mr. Wiley was snoring in his bed. He had finished his evening's work, if it was fair to call it that, about an hour before. Now he lay on his back with a blinder over his eyes, having just entered into an early stage of REM sleep. An acute listener in the room might have heard the start of a tick-tick-ticking noise, very much like the sound of a fishing reel being reeled in. Then the two top corners of his blanket started slowly rising. Though Mr. Wiley was very much mentally somewhere else—in fact, at that moment, being chased across the plains by a posse and outrunning them on his trusted old mustang—he felt a slight chill on his upper body. He reached up and grabbed the blanket and pulled it down. Interestingly, the sound of a fishing reel unwinding followed the sheet down. Secure again with his blanket, he rolled over onto his side and tried to resume his escape from the posse.

A few minutes later, having given the posse the slip, he was relaxing in a cantina on the other side of the Rio Grande with a friendly señorita. Again, his cozy, warm blanket began to levitate. This time it rose about three feet before he grabbed it and yanked it back down. He rolled over in the other direction and tried to find the pretty señorita again. After two more of these interruptions, even in his dream his irritation rose to anger.

Meanwhile, one floor below and one room over, something similar was taking place. In the darkness of his room, Sergeant Snipe was also dreaming about being south of the border, but he was considerably farther south—all the way to Nicaragua— and it was about a century later. He wasn't frivolously whiling away his time in a cantina chasing a pretty señorita either. He was cunningly prowling the jungle on the trail of some murderous, drug-pushing, orphan-making revolutionaries. At first, when his blanket began to float, he didn't let it distract him. But after Fast and Easy got tired of holding up the two corners of the blanket three feet in the air, they began to shake their fishing poles. Sergeant Snipe felt a breeze kicking up in the jungle. He quickly snatched down his blanket and continued his Nicaraguan pursuit, ready and on the lookout.

By the third time, he was up to his limit with distractions. Deep in sleep, it seemed he was surrounded; there must have been thirty or forty of them. He reached under his pillow and pulled out his government-issue Glock 9mm special edition and fired three shots through the blanket into the ceiling. Fast and Easy ripped their lines from the blanket, and it floated back down as they took off with their poles out the balcony door. The malefactors having abandoned their ambuscade, Sergeant Snipe resumed his trek through the jungle. Even if Easy and Fast had stayed around long enough, they probably wouldn't have noticed that Sergeant Snipe's pistol was not the typical handgun of a noncommissioned Special Forces officer.

At almost the exact same time, from the floor above, another shot rang out. Mr. Wiley had tolerated long enough the distractions to his wooing of the Mexican maiden. He had drawn his pearl-handled Colt six-shooter from under his pillow and fired a shot. One shot was enough. The blanket floated back down as Dolphin and Claudette hightailed it with their poles, out and down the balcony.

A few moments later, Ms. Root and Mr. Mallow, with pistols similar to Sergeant Snipe's drawn, were peering out a window in the second-floor hallway. Mr. Wiley walked down the stairs, his right hand behind his back, "I think someone just attempted to burgle me," he said, noticing their pistols but keeping his own behind his back.

"We saw them getting away," said Ms. Root, peering again out the window. "There was at least two of them."

"Burglars my eye!" Sergeant Snipe said, walking out of his room. Fortunately, he had put on his trousers. "They were peepers."

"Well then, they were peeper burglars," said Mr. Wiley. "It appears one needs to be vigilant around here."

Just then, Dolphin and Bertram came up the hall. "Did I hear gunshots?" asked Dolphin.

"Burglar perverts," said Mr. Wiley. "There's burglar perverts on the prowl. Not a whole lot of honest thieves anymore. It's a sign of the times. And where's that director of security of yours? That boy's been sleeping on the job."

CHAPTER 32

The next morning, while Lunch was cooking breakfast, Dolphin called a meeting in the kitchen.

"We still have three days," said Dolphin. "I think at least they're starting to have some doubts about the place."

"I'm starting to have some doubts about *them*," said Fast. "All four of them are packing artillery. We almost got shot last night."

"They're from the South, or three of them are, anyway," said Claudette.

"Okay, we have three days to get them out of here," said Dolphin. "Any ideas, anyone?"

"Just no more of that ghost stuff," said Lunch. "That's my only idea."

"It didn't work anyway," said Fast. "They thought our ghosts were robbers."

"I'm glad I wasn't working Snipe's blanket," said Claudette. "Tight-whites gross me out."

"He did have a few cool tattoos," Easy said.

"Ideas," said Dolphin. "I need ideas."

"We could smoke them out," said Fast.

"And then Aunt Clemmie wouldn't kill Dolphin for renting the house," said Claudette. "She would kill him for wrecking it."

"Good point," said Fast.

"Let's take the money and run," said Lunch, who was feeling considerably more himself after Dolphin had told him that the story about the house was part of the plan all along. "We'll be like Butch Cassidy and the Sundance Kid, and we'll go to Argentina. I doubt your aunt would look for us down there."

"Of course she would," said Claudette. "She's one of the world authorities on Butch and Sundance. She has a whole book about their techniques in robbing trains, and a whole section on their thieving in Argentina. I know—I've read it."

"You guys are a great help," said Dolphin, beginning to pace the floor. "This is going to have to be drastic, and I know you guys aren't going to like it, but I can't think of anything else."

"What aren't we going to like?" asked Fast.

"Using the Idiots."

"We're going to use the Idiots?" asked Easy.

"Yep. The patrons already think there's burglars around here that are trying to rob them, right? And Mr. Wiley said it was intolerable. And we weren't even trying to rob them. Well, the crime situation in Tranquility Beach is just going to get worse, and for their own safety, and so I don't get sued—I'll tell them that's what my lawyer told me—they're going to just have to flee. 'Cause there's going to be more robbers afoot."

"Robbers afoot?" asked Lunch.

"Yes. Robbers afoot. And we're going to recruit Crazy Ahab and the Village Idiots to be the robbers."

"Dude, that sounds awesome," said Easy, who hadn't been home to check for messages on his answering machine since his earlier one from Julia.

CHAPTER 33

That night, the bells on the grandfather clock in the Maison's living room had just finished their twelfth toll. The house was now dark and quiet. Mr. Wiley had retired early, saying he was still distracted from last night's incident. Ms. Root, the last of the patrons to turn in, had done so more than an hour earlier. Outside, the storm having passed, all was peaceful and still. That is, excepting the three black-clad figures who crept up the outside stairs, which lead to the balconies of the second and third floors. One of the figures was tall and thin, another short and plump, and the third somewhat average in stature, though not in character. Each had his hair stuffed into a dark stocking cap, and their faces were smeared with black shoe polish their leader had procured from his father's shoeshine kit.

Upon reaching the second-floor balcony, the three figures dispersed toward the three doors that opened onto the balcony. The tall, thin figure slithered toward the northernmost door, which led into Mr. Mallow's room. The pudgy figure tiptoed to the southernmost door, leading to where Sergeant Snipe reposed.

And Crazy Ahab crept toward the middle door, behind which Ms. Root was getting her rest.

Moments earlier, Aunt Clemmie's taxi, after having dropped Julia off at her apartment, arrived at the Maison. Not wanting to awaken Dolphin, Aunt Clemmie had left her luggage at the hanger in which Mr. Allen was keeping his plane for the night. She would send Dolphin to pick it up in the morning. It being 3:00 a.m., New York time, she couldn't wait to climb into her own bed.

Not wanting to disturb Louis, who was fast asleep in her arms, she refrained from turning on the lights as she began her trudge up the three flights of stairs to her room. As she approached her bedroom, she didn't notice the light that dimly shone from under its door.

By this time, Crazy Ahab and the two Idiots had opened the balcony doors with the keys Dolphin had given them and were creeping into each bedroom. Dolphin's plan to get Ahab and the Idiots to burgle the Sandcastle had needed some measure of refinement after he thought it through. He decided to tell Ahab and his friends that three college girls were staying in the rooms, and he wanted Ahab and the Idiots to pull off a panty raid. Ahab and the Idiots had never done one of these before, but they had heard that in former days it was something the college fraternities used to do to sororities, and it sounded way cool. They took Dolphin's offer as a peacemaking gesture.

Dolphin had instructed them that once they were inside the rooms, they should go to the dressers, find whatever they could, and then scatter out of there.

As Ahab and the Idiots were approaching Mr. Mallow's, Sergeant Snipe's, and Ms. Root's dressers, Aunt Clemmie opened the door to her bedroom. What she saw was a middle-aged man, wearing a Dallas Cowboys baseball cap, standing beside her bed, on which a large open suitcase rested. The man was packing up an electronic device of some sort. A scream that could not be characterized as moderate shook the house.

Mr. Wiley froze for a moment as the woman dug into her purse. The firmly built matron with red hair who had just startled a few years off his life looked familiar to him. Then he recalled the face from the dust jackets of some of his favorite books. Was she on his trail too?

Aunt Clemmie dropped Louis, who ran quickly out of the room, and pulled from her purse a snub-nose .38, which she was licensed to carry, for as she often said, paraphrasing Chesterton, "Who knows what danger lurks on any street corner?" She pointed the gun at Mr. Wiley and said, "Reach for the sky."

Mr. Wiley responded by pulling from the back of his belt a Colt .45 revolver, long barreled, with a pearl handle. It was quite a contrast in pistols, one extremely long, the other extremely short. He carried his to honor Jesse James, who was a distant relative and something of a role model. She carried hers, humbly paying homage to one of her favorite characters from her own books, "Wild Ann Wong, the Chinese Revenger."

"Love your writing, Ms. Hardin, but I reckon we're in what you'd call a Mexican standoff," Mr. Wiley said.

Seven gunshots rang out below, followed by a stampede of feet on the balcony and down the stairs. Four more shots followed.

At the distraction, Mr. Wiley put his pistol in his belt, closed and took up his suitcase, and darted past Aunt Clemmie toward the main stairs.

Aunt Clemmie let him pass, not about to shoot one of her

book-buying fans and thinking there was something about the gentleman that was likable enough.

Fortunately or unfortunately, depending on whose perspective you are taking, Dolphin had just come out of his room on the first floor and was peeking up the circular stairway, trying to see just how badly his plan had gone wrong. Suddenly, the force of a tornado in the form of a suitcase and a cap-wearing, middle-aged, well-built Texan slammed into him. Then darkness enveloped the earth.

CHAPTER 34

When Dolphin came to, thirty seconds or so later, the first thing he saw was Sergeant Snipe, Mr. Mallow, and Ms. Root each holding dull black automatic pistols, the latter also holding a large Colt revolver. At first, he thought they were pointed at him. Then he thought they were pointed at Mr. Wiley, who was lying unconscious next to him at the foot of the stairs. But then he realized they were pointed farther up the stairs. His eyes drew up, first seeing the thick legs, then the wide hips, then a snub-nose revolver, then they rested on the person—of his aunt. And she was pointing her revolver at the three conscious patrons. If there hadn't been so much hardware pointed about, he might have thought about making a run for it.

"What is the meaning of this?" Aunt Clemmie demanded with authority.

"I can explain everything," Dolphin said, actually able to explain little.

"I wasn't talking to you, meathead," Aunt Clemmie said. "You'll have more than that to do later."

"If you lower your weapon, Ms. Hardin, I will explain," Ms. Root said.

"I'll do nothing of the sort," said Aunt Clemmie. "I am licensed for this weapon, and you stand in my house, uninvited."

"Not exactly, Auntie," said Dolphin.

"Randolph, please desist. You're obviously out of your mind."

"Auntie, it's all my fault. I'll pay everyone back, someday. I'll get a job."

"Silence!" she commanded.

Just then Claudette burst into the room in her bathrobe with her hair down, not looking very much like a male butler. "It's my fault," she said, kneeling at Dolphin's side and helping him to sit up. "I'll help him pay everyone back. I'll get a job too."

"You! What are you doing here?" demanded Aunt Clemmie.

"I was the butler."

"I liked him better then," said Ms. Root.

"Someone tell me what is going on here," Aunt Clemmie ordered.

"I'm Special Agent Root of the FBI, and your nephew has just captured the number four man on our most-wanted list."

"I'm Special Agent Snipe of the Secret Service, ma'am. It's true. Without your nephew we would have never got him."

"I'm Marshall Mallow of the IRS. I don't know if it's true we would have never got him, but he . . ."

"My nephew? I don't believe it."

"Got who?" asked Dolphin.

"Him," said Sergeant Snipe, pointing to Mr. Wiley, who was starting to stir. "He was number three on the Secret Service's list."

"He was number 362 on the IRS's," said Mr. Mallow.

"We've been after him for over three years," said Ms. Root. "He would have gotten away but for young Smoote's tackling him as he tried to escape."

"Number four on the FBI's most-wanted list?" said Aunt Clemmie, uncocking her pistol and thinking. "That would be William James, also known as Wiley Bill Gibbons, as I recall."

"Exactly," said Ms. Root. "Also known as William Wiley, the worst electronic funds thief of all time. We finally caught up with him when he rented a room here."

"Auntie, I rented out the house," said Dolphin. "You people are all going to have to leave. There will be refunds. It just might take a while."

"I never stole a penny," protested Wiley Bill, alias Mr. Wiley, who had come to consciousness and immediately reached for the suitcase he had been trying to escape with. "And that's a fact."

"Likely story. You don't expect us to believe that," said Mr. Mallow, who then reeled off the Miranda Code to Wiley Bill.

"Oh, shut up," said Aunt Clemmie. "I know this case, and if you blockheaded bureaucrats had bothered to consult me, you might have solved it years ago."

"We're aware of your credentials, Ms. Smoote," said Ms. Root. "But we have had the best minds in the government working this case."

"Then you should know that what he says is technically true," said Aunt Clemmie.

"We know he has amassed a fortune of over one hundred million dollars and has not paid a penny of income tax on it," said Mr. Mallow, "by somehow tapping into the electronic funds transfer system."

"Tax evasion would have been enough to arrest him," Ms.

Root said, "but it was imperative we learn *how* he was doing it. And now, with what we have here in that luggage he is hugging, we should be able to figure that out and put him away for a long time."

Aunt Clemmie lowered her pistol and walked the rest of the way down the stairs. "Usually when a criminal rationalizes his crime, it is hogwash. But in this case, he is telling the truth. He doesn't steal the money. He just borrows it. That is why he has been so difficult for you to catch."

"It is true we don't know how he does it," said Sergeant Snipe. "But here, staying in the house, I was able to partially tap into his system. In a few more days, I think I would have figured it out."

"We have him for tax evasion, anyway," said Mr. Mallow. "Just like Al Capone."

"Oh, he's nothing like Al Capone," said Aunt Clemmie. "And I wouldn't pay my taxes, or at least not the excessive ones, if I could get away with it."

"How do you know so much about this?" asked Claudette.

"She's probably writing a book about it," said Dolphin.

"To honor me with a book by you would be of some condolence," said Mr. Wiley. "I recognized you from your book covers. I am a big fan."

"I would love to write it, someday, but I still need a few more facts. The First Security Bank of Seattle, who at first was hit very hard by your scheme, hired me to see if I could solve why they were missing something around twenty-seven thousand dollars in interest on their assets every night of the business week. A number of very wealthy and influential people have considerable amounts in that bank, and they demanded a professional investigation. I discovered the trick two years ago."

"So, it was you?" said Wiley Bill. "I noticed the slight reduction right away. But what was twenty-seven thousand a night with what I was making at other banks."

"It was a brilliant scheme, Mr. James, I must admit," said Aunt Clemmie. "Undoubtably, your great-great-uncle Jesse would be proud of you. If you had just paid your taxes, it might be all they could get on you. They don't have laws yet for electronically borrowing money."

"I don't pay any taxes," said Dolphin.

"That's because you don't make any money," said Aunt Clemmie.

"I'm going to make a note to have you audited," said Mr. Mallow to Dolphin.

"Mr. James in fact did merely borrow the money," Aunt Clemmie went on. "Every night he would tap into the electronic funds transfer system through a backdoor hole he built while he was the manager of information technology at Longhorn City Bank in Austin, Texas. I never bothered to investigate where he got his technical expertise."

"He got his start in the Marines," said Ms. Root, "where he was one of their most brilliant battlefield communications specialists. From there he went to NASA in Houston to work on the Space Shuttle communications systems. And from there to the bank, where I am sure they were delighted—for a while anyway—to have such a technical wizard working for them. Agent Snipe has been able to tap into a portion of Wiley's homemade mini microwave transceiver and was making progress toward the solution. He got his start with the Marines too."

"Semper fi, bro," said Mr. Wiley. "At least it was one of us."

"Sorry," said Sergeant Snipe.

"Which now you can legally confiscate," added Aunt Clemmie. "But you really didn't need his equipment to figure out how he was doing it. Once he tapped into the system, and with what he learned at the bank on how to unscramble the encryption, he would divert streams of digital money to one of his own numbered accounts in the Caribbean or Switzerland. Many trillions of dollars are transferred every workday night. He would only divert a relatively small amount—ten billion or so a night—and he would only divert it for a few hours. Then he would send the digital stream of money on to where it was originally supposed to go. So, literally, he was only borrowing the money. But the interest on ten billion dollars, even for two hours, can add up quickly. He wasn't greedy—the downfall of most thieves—but he could easily bank for himself thousands of dollars a night. I congratulate you, Mr. James. You would do your great ancestor proud."

"So, that's how he did it," said Mr. Mallow. "William, it *was* brilliant, but you can't outfox the taxman."

"Why didn't the bank in Seattle have him arrested?" asked Claudette, who was thrilled getting so close to such a case.

"First, banks are extremely careful about negative publicity. A bank, and the banking system for that matter, cannot survive without the confidence of the public. They couldn't afford to have it known that their system had been breached. There are in fact numerous incidents of banking crimes that have gone unpublicized because of the potential negative impact. Second, they tried to apprehend him privately, but he was on the lam, as they say. Even I didn't know where he was—if I did know, I would have been obligated to turn him in. But tracking criminals is not strictly my forte. I'll stick to writing their stories."

"He was on the move in a boat most of the time," said Sergeant Snipe. "Sailing the seven seas, with that comms system he built. I have to admit his hardware and software are something else. He'd never be in one place long enough for us to triangulate on him. His boat broke down, and that's how he ended up here, renting a room. It was because of that leaky sailboat that we got him."

"And the excellent work of you nephew," said Ms. Root. "And may I say, we had a delightful time here. Your nephew and his friends have been such delightful hosts. That story he told the other night—I nearly split a gut. It was such a hoot I almost died trying not to laugh. I do hope you'll write it. I want to tell it someday to my children—if I ever have any."

"You might have thought *parts* of it were funny," said Mr. Wiley, "but you can't tell me those weren't real tears you were crying when old Kari—or whatever her name was—died."

"Well it's true, parts of it were quite moving," said Ms. Root.

"I didn't think it was so funny," said Mr. Mallow. "I couldn't sleep and even had this dream about old Lightning and Thunder trying to steal my blanket."

"You told a story, funny, scary, and which also moved this woman to tears?" said Aunt Clemmie. "You really aren't nearly the blockhead you let on to be. But you must develop your talent. Which does bring us to the issue. Did I hear that you rented out this house?"

"I did, Auntie," said Dolphin. "It didn't seem so ill-advised at the time."

"How many times have I told you that rationalizing your crimes is what criminals do?"

"You're right. You all," said Dolphin to the patrons, "are going to have to move out. This place really belongs to my aunt. I hope you can cut me a little slack on the time I need to pay you back?"

"I am afraid that will be impossible," said Mr. Mallow. "The government is scrupulous in these procedures. They'll want a strict accounting of every penny we've spent here, and a full refund on rent unused."

"Couldn't you just wait a little? I'm going to have to find a job," said Dolphin.

"So will I," said Claudette.

"I will too," said Lunch, coming into the living room from around the corner, where he had been listening.

"Us too," said Easy, as he and Fast walked in from the kitchen.

"I am afraid the government is very inflexible," said Mr. Mallow. "We will need the refund by the time we send in our expense reports, and if we haven't done that in two months, we will not be remunerated. And then we will have to press charges."

"My bloodline has finally got to me. I'm a criminal and going to jail," said Dolphin.

"Just hold your horses a minute," said Ms. Root, giving Dolphin a cheering smile. "Within two months you should be one of the wealthiest unemployed surf bums in Tranquility Beach. Ample time for you to give us our refunds."

"And you deserve it, son," said Agent Snipe. "You've been through a lot. I'm even going to leave you a can of the jungle juice, just in case you get bothered by that red tide again. And by the way, sorry we didn't catch those burglars, but I don't think they'll be back. We chased them up the beach a bit but thought we ought to get back here and keep our eye on Wiley Bill. It appears he had caught on to us and was trying to make his break tonight. But you didn't let that happen."

"How did you finally figure out who we were, Bill?" asked Ms. Root.

"I saw your guns. All three of you had Glock nines," said Wiley Bill. "Those are government pieces: FBI and Secret Service issue. Knew something was up when I saw those last night."

"Wealthy! Did someone say I'm going to be wealthy? How am I going to be wealthy?"

"Why, the reward! You don't know about the reward, do you?" said Ms. Root.

"Ah . . . no," said Dolphin, feeling better all of a sudden.

"By golly, he was just doing his duty out of civic-mindedness" said Agent Snipe. "He's a true American."

"There's a one-hundred-thousand-dollar reward for 'information leading to, or aiding in, the capture and arrest of the E-Funds Bandit,' which there is no doubt you are fully entitled to," said Ms. Root.

"You will be paying taxes on it, of course," said Mr. Mallow. "And a few special ones apply to this kind of thing. But when we're done with you, you should still be getting thirty-seven or thirty-eight thousand out of it. And after you've paid us back, including what you owe Wiley Bill—for despite being a criminal, his rights are still protected—you should have three or four thousand left over."

"That's what you think, you sniveling thief," said Aunt Clemmie. "Excessive taxation is an impingement on the freedom this country was born on. I'll set my tax people on it right away, Randolph. We'll amortize the value of the Sandcastle and at its current value, you'll get a big write-off. And that will only be the beginning. When they're done, you'll get ninety percent. I do hope you kept the receipts."

"Every one of them," said Claudette.

Lunch started rubbing his hands together, saying, "Delightful, delightful."

Fast and Easy joined in, saying, "Delightful, awesomely delightful."

It was here that Dolphin definitely confused his friends. Maybe it was from the knock on his head he got when Mr. Wiley bowled into him. Maybe it was that Aunt Clemmie's influence on him was starting to come out more. Maybe it was that he had got his radical style (though not his casual style) back, in a somewhat demented fashion. Nevertheless, he thought it over for a few seconds then simply smiled and said, "Well, Time's flailing his scythe, and I need to get to work."

EPILOGUE

In the end, after Aunt Clemmie's accountants got to work too, Dolphin netted more than $87,000 of the reward money. These were some of the same accountants who do the books for the movie studios, which manage to show losses on $400 million–grossing movies. Only special people, like Aunt Clemmie, get access to them. He would have received more, but the tax system is not kind to unmarried males.

Wiley Bill James graciously said he didn't care about his unused rent being refunded. He had more than enough money, and where he had it stashed, no one was going to find it. Dolphin paid back the three governmental renters, had the Sandcastle walls patched and painted from the gunshot holes, had all the locks on the doors changed (seeing as how the Idiots now had keys), bought a high-tech video-based security system that Sergeant Snipe advised him on, and still had well over $60,000 left.

He stuck to the original plan. He split it, saving half for himself and divided the other half four ways, Lunch, Easy, Fast, and Claudette each getting an equal share. Aunt Clemmie made

Dolphin put half his money in with one of her investment managers, to which he agreed without a fight. He felt he was still on thin ice with her, and he really didn't need all the money at the time, anyway. They all had more than enough to go to the Islands that winter, and that is exactly what they planned to do. All of them except Claudette, that is.

On the night of the capture of Wiley Bill, something strange really must have happened to Dolphin. Perhaps it was that bump on the head. Perhaps it was the heady experience of the G-men—or G-people, if you will—saying that he was a hero. Perhaps it was the flattering remarks that were shared about his story of SC Parker and the ghosts. Whatever the cause, his creative mind had started working. *So, I get credit for the capture of Wiley Bill*, he thought. Ms. Root had said that. *Then*, he further reasoned, *everything that happened around here in the last few weeks—I technically own the rights to it, including the story part of it.*

"Now you're thinking, my boy!" Aunt Clemmie had later confirmed when Dolphin put it before her. As an author, she continually mulled over similar issues of intellectual property rights.

This was what Dolphin was alluding to when he exclaimed "I need to get to work." He was going to write up this adventure and start his career as an author. For somehow he had got the ridiculous notion that writing wasn't really the same as work, or at least wasn't hard work. Oh, that naive child!

Claudette did her best to be happy with his plan but then became very happy when Dolphin asked her to be his writing partner. She expressed her gratitude by giving him a big kiss.

And that brings us to why Claudette ended up not traveling with the Dawgs that winter. Dolphin and she had been trying to make progress on the story for a couple of weeks. But it seemed that Dolphin's work habits weren't quite jibing with Claudette's, and neither were their aesthetics, which was the thing that eventually caused the rupture, or at least the temporary rupture, in their relationship.

Dolphin tended to opt for a much looser writing style and for less grammatical precision. Claudette was already quite irritated after Dolphin had missed two days in a row of their daily three-hour writing sessions—the surf had been particularly good that week. When Dolphin was two hours late the third day, her frustration peaked. They soon got into an argument about a turn of phrase. They started saying mean things to each other like, "You don't know the difference between a predicate nominative and a direct object." That's what Claudette said. And Dolphin said, "Who cares? Neither do most Americans who went to public school."

After a few rounds of this sort of verbal abuse, they decided that maybe it wasn't a great idea for two artists such as they to write together, at least for the time being. Dolphin said she could write her own version of the story, and he would write his.

Aunt Clemmie forgave Dolphin for renting out the Sandcastle. She said there were some parts of the idea that were quite creative. She liked the butler bit, and for some reason she thought the idea of Lunch Biggunes as the cook was brilliant. She became friends with Lunch and started to invite him over to barbeque for her on festive occasions, or just when she felt bored. She said talking to Lunch tended to spur her imagination and give her a different perspective on the criminal mind.

She was most pleased, however, with her budding relationship with Wiley Bill James. They hit it off immediately. Bill offered her exclusive rights to his life story, and she of course was thrilled with the opportunity. She has yet to settle on a title but is toying with something like *Borrowing a Billion: The Life of Wiley Bill James.*

She helped Wiley Bill get the slimiest, slipperiest lawyer in North America, and Bill ended up striking a deal with the feds to share all he knew about electronic borrowing and electronic thievery. So, in the end, Bill only had to do a year and a half in prison, and that in Folsom prison, where Johnny Cash made such a great album. It wasn't Texas, but it was almost like going home.

When Claudette had to go back to Oklahoma to visit her ailing grandmother, she and Dolphin decided they should put their relationship on hold for a while. And Dolphin even took a break from dating altogether. It seemed that as soon as he made that decision, his cool and casual came roaring back, strong as ever. He couldn't keep the birds away. Of course, it could have been because he was now also rich. Anyway, after a while he dated some but didn't get attached. Claudette still lingered in his mind.

ACKNOWLEDGMENTS

I grew up close to the beach in Southern California in an era when the coolest thing in the world was to be a hot surfer. It was cooler than being a star athlete, a rock star, even a movie star, and way cooler than being a writer. The cool surf crowd would have thought writers nerdy, at least writers who weren't also good surfers. My attempt has been to entertain the reader with a little of what it was like back then. Admittedly, in some of the parts the truth has been a bit hyperbolized, but not much regarding the "style" issues and that, to avoid gainful employment, any surfer worth his huarache sandals would do almost anything. Which brings me to the *crime* part of the story. The concept of some high-tech "borrowing" of money from the nightly electronic transfer flows is absolutely true. I can't tell you how I know this, but Aunt Clemmie knows.

A good friend has a house on the Strand, and it is this house that the "Sandcastle" is modeled after. It was built in the late 1920s and really does not have a perpendicular angle in any of its walls. Many thanks to him for the inspiration of his domicile.

Thanks to CB, TA, DJ, DJ, MJ, DA, JR, LP, CS, and AB, who acted in a very early version of this story when friends and I decided to do a movie over a four-day Thanksgiving weekend. And a special thanks to by surfer buddy Rob Gira, who gave me good counsel regarding the great legendary surfer honored in the ghost story section my novel .

The literary influences are many but chiefly P. G. Wodehouse (fairly obvious) and G. K. Chesterton. If the reader has not encountered these masters, I encourage her or him to do so.

Finally, I'd like to thank my editors Joy Jacobson and Michael Krohn, and also the many people at Blackstone Publishing, too many to mention, for all the support, encouragement, and courtesy.

J3